THE DEATH OF BROCELIANDE

THE DEATH OF BROCELIANDE

BRIAN STABLEFORD

WILDSIDE PRESS

For Daisy and Chloe

I

The Iron-master and his Family

There was once an iron-master named Ernand whose foundry was in a vast clearing in the great highland forest, close to quarries from which iron ore was extracted, and surrounded by a village where the workers in those various enterprises lived.

There was also a mine nearby from which copper ores were derived, the produce of which Ernand combined with tin to make bronze. It was in bronze that he still founded cannon and bells, as his father had done before him, but since inheriting the foundry he had been much more prolific in his use of iron, with which he made horseshoes, the heads of axes, the blades of weapons, barrel-hoops, wheel-rims and all kinds of agricultural implements, especially heavy plowshares; that was what entitled him to claim the title of iron-master, which was recent in honor, if not in origin.

Ernand's foundry was situated beside a road that cut straight through the heart of the forest. In one direction it led straight to a busy port, via a sizeable town; in the other it forked not far beyond the foundry, the left-hand fork veering downhill toward the plain, and the capital city of the region, whereas the more steeply-angled right fork soon gave rise to further branches that extended up into the mountains and the highest regions of the forest. The main road was well-made and well-maintained, bedded on gravel and paved with stone, in order to support the heavy carts that transported goods to and from the port to the inland town and all the way to the capital. It also conveyed all of Ernand's products to his widely-scattered clients and markets.

Ernand considered himself to be a great pioneer of industry and tool-making, and firmly believed that the future of humankind depended on iron and its many uses. In mastering iron, Ernand believed, he was playing his part in the human mastery of the world.

By virtue of that belief, Ernand was deeply disappointed when his only son, Alastor, grew up with a deep distaste for iron, and even for bronze, and was firmly determination not to follow in his father's footsteps. It was not that the boy was not industrious, but that his interests and his talents were all turned toward wood and its many employments. That was perhaps not unnatural in a boy brought up in a village surrounded by a great forest, all the more so as his mother, Eulalie, was a child of that forest, the daughter of a widowed woodcutter and charcoal-burner who supplied fuel for Ernand's furnaces. It did not seem so very natural to Ernand, however, to whom Alastor was a profound disappointment.

Ernand's conviction that his son's antipathy to iron had something unnatural about it was encouraged, and intensified over time, by a rumor that was current in the region regarding Eulalie, his wife. Although the woodcutter was absolutely adamant that she was his daughter, the gossip of the old crones of the village suggested that she was, in fact, a changeling that had been slyly introduced into the actual daughter's cradle by the fae-folk, and that it was the presence of the changeling in her home that had caused the premature death of the woodcutter's wife, Eulalie's mother.

Ernand had first fallen in love with Eulalie when he was still a relatively young man, who had only just inherited the foundry from his father, and she was only sixteen years old. He had treated such tales as nonsense, and continued to do so. He insisted on believing—contrary to the vast majority of the residents of the forest—that the fae-folk were entirely imaginary, the product of a primitive imagination that should have been disciplined long ago, by religion if not by skeptical philosophy. Although Eulalie married him very willingly, however, rather than merely being bartered in marriage for the sake of vulgar interest by her parents, as was common among townsfolk, she certainly did not have her husband's love of iron, and could never be persuaded to acquire it. Indeed, it sometimes seemed that she suffered from contact with the metal—something that only encouraged the old crones' gossip, because that aversion was held by legend to be typical of the fae-folk.

Eulalie's health was always fragile, even before she married Ernand, but it remained sturdy enough for her to bear him two children, Alastor being followed after an interval of two years by a daughter named Catrianne, before she perished not long after the birth of the latter. In view of that circumstance, Alastor's antipathy to the material of his father's industry could not be attributed to any direct influence of his mother, whom he had hardly known, but one belief Ernand shared with the crones was that such tendencies were in the blood, and needed no particular education to bring them out.

Because of her sex, Catrianne could hardly have been expected to devote herself to any kind of laborious industry, let alone that of ironworking, but she too was something of a disappointment to Ernand, because she loved her brother dearly and supported him in everything, including his resistance to Ernand's attempts to direct his interests and shape him for a career identical to his own. As the differences between the father and the son gradually developed from mutual incomprehension to open conflict, Catrianne always lent Alastor substantial reinforcement in arguments that eventually took on the proportions of verbal battles.

Catrianne too had an aversion for iron, which extended even to the employment of needles, and instead of developing the skills in needlework that would normally have been expected of a female child of her class, as necessary training for marriage and housekeeping, she concentrated her time and interest the development of her musical skills. She played all manner of wind and stringed instruments with consummate skill. Partly by virtue of her interest, Alastor developed a particular interest in using his woodworking skills in the manufacture of musical instruments of both kinds.

That specialism caused further irritation to Ernand, who might have been able to understand and tolerate his son's art had it been applied primarily to the manufacture of the wooden components of tools, weapons, wheels or barrels, or even to the kinds of carpentry associated with the building of houses and cabinet-making; but he regarded music and all its associated instruments as impractical frippery.

As tensions built up in their home, Alastor and Catrianne, even as children, began spending much of the day in the forest, exploring it and learning about the plants that grew there and the animals that lived there, in spite of the real dangers still posed by some of those animals, including wild pigs, wolves and bears. In the parts of the great forest that extended into valleys, aristocrats sometimes hunted such animals, but hunters rarely came far into the highlands, where the ground was too rugged once the horses left the road. They preferred in any case to chase roe deer, which were less dangerous when cornered than pigs, let alone wolves or bears.

When the time came for Alastor to begin work, he left his father's house in order to go to the town on the road to the port, where he was apprenticed to an aging maker of musical instruments named Zebedee. At first, however, he returned every Sunday in order to see Catrianne, with whom he went to mass at the village church and then went walking in the woods. Their separation did not last long, however, and as soon as Alastor was able to afford accommodation that she could share, Catrianne came to join him in the town. Alastor's skill had quickly become well-known and greatly appreciated, and the demand for musical instruments was too considerable for his aging master—whose fingers were beginning to suffer from arthritis—to execute more than a small fraction of the commissions he received. Zebedee was a good and honest man, who lived very frugally, and who allowed Alastor to receive and keep a larger share of the money earned by his labor than many a master would have done.

Zebedee's reputation extended beyond the town in which he worked, and when Alastor began to do take over the greater part of their collective employment, he not only acquired a share of that renown but further increased it. Before long, he was obtaining requests to purchase instruments, and commissions to make them, from the port and from towns and villages inland of the foundry, including some in the elevated regions of the highlands, where the forest extended all the way to the tree-line of the mountains. For that reason, he often traveled on horseback along the road, and sometimes along the winding side-paths that led into the upper highlands. He always stopped at the foundry whenever he passed through the village, even though his father did not seem enthusiastic to receive his visits.

On one occasion, Alastor received a commission directed specifically to him, to make an unusual instrument based on a very ancient design, which came from a remote hamlet high in the mountains. On his way to deliver the instrument he called, as usual, on his father, and asked him whether he had ever heard of the hamlet in question.

"Aye," said Ernand, "I have. It has a bad reputation, because of a witch who's said to live in the neighborhood, who steals children and teaches them to sing like birds."

"That's a very strange thing for a witch to do," observed Alastor. "Where does she take the children."

"Oh, she leaves them at home with their parents, and only steals their souls. When they grow up, she lets them alone. The lads go to work and the lasses marry, like normal folk, but she steals their own children in their time."

"If all witches are as harmless as that," Alastor said, "I wonder why the church persecutes them."

"You'll have to ask the curé about that," Ernand grunted. "It's no business of mine."

Alastor continued on his way, taking the right fork in the road and going high into the mountains. He was so late returning from that expedition, however, that Zebedee and Catrianne became convinced that he had been overtaken by misfortune, especially when they heard a rumor that a terrible storm had raged in the mountains during the night when he ought to have reached the hamlet, which the local people naturally blamed on the malevolence of the local witch.

Several days passed after the date when Alastor should have returned, and Catrianne was about to put on mourning-dress, when he reappeared abruptly, riding a horse that was not his own, and carrying on its rump a slender girl, seemingly no more than sixteen years old. As soon as they had dismounted, he introduced her to his sister by the name of Lucinia, and declared that he intended to marry her as soon as possible.

That news deflected interrogations as to precisely what had happened during the delay to Alastor's return, and the explanations he gave were sketchy, although the implication was that the missing days had been taken up by his rapid courtship. He told Zebedee and Catrianne that he had gone astray during the storm after being thrown from his horse, which had bolted. Left limping, he had been forced to seek hospitality wherever he could, which was not easy in the high forest. Lucinia and her mother had kindly taken him in, and had kept him until his bruises had healed and he was able to ride again. They had also given him a horse, and, because he had fallen in love with Lucinia in the interim, he had asked her to come with him to the town. She had agreed, and her mother had given her permission.

The formalities of the marriage might have proved a trifle awkward, because Lucinia had no documentation of her civil estate and had never been baptized. She explained to the Maire of the town, however, that her parents were mountain-dwellers descended from nomads, who paid little attention to such formalities, and the Maire kindly made no difficulty about the civil registration of the marriage. The local curé was perfectly happy to carry out a belated baptism in order that the religious component of the alliance could proceed with equal propriety.

After the marriage, Alastor's affairs prospered, as he gradually took over almost all the work that Zebedee had previously done, and his own reputation as a constructor of beautiful musical instruments continued to increase. He was soon able to buy a house large enough to accommodate the family that he and Lucinia hoped to have—she was already pregnant with her first child—and also for Catrianne, from whom there was never any possibility of his separating.

Catrianne had initially experienced some slight distress in consequence of the intrusion into their home of a newcomer, but she soon came to like Lucinia very much, and a firm alliance was forged between them almost immediately, because Lucinia sang beautifully, and loved to sing, especially to the accompaniment of Catrianne's flutes and lutes. Although Lucinia was an inept player of such instruments by comparison with Catrianne, she was familiar with an abundance of tunes completely unknown to the iron-master's daughter, which she delighted in teaching her sister-in-law to play—a delight redoubled by the fact that Catrianne was able to play them so beautifully that she seemed to add extra charm and meaning to them.

The sound of Lucinia singing to the tune of one or other of Catrianne's instruments—all products of Alastor's artistry, naturally—soon became so familiar to the household's new neighbors that they nicknamed Lucinia "the Nightingale." She did not like the nickname, though, which seemed to have some unfortunate connotation for her, and she was always eager to tell anyone prepared to listen that she did not warrant it. If anyone were entitled to it, she sometimes said, it was Catrianne, because the notes she produced on her various instruments were more closely akin to beautiful birdsong than the sounds produced by her own human larynx. Few people agreed though, and insisted on believing that Lucinia was merely being modest.

The three of them lived together very happily—which was as well, given that Catrianne had no desire to leave the household. Although more than one suitor had previously expressed an interest in going to the foundry and confronting the redoubtable iron-master in order to ask for her hand, she had put them off gently, explaining that she had no desire as yet to be anyone's wife. That determination was not altered by the advent of Lucinia, and seemed to become even firmer when, a year after the marriage, not long after they had moved to the new house, Lucinia gave birth to a son, and firmer still a year after that, when she gave birth to a daughter.

Catrianne seemed to regard the children as her own as much as Alastor's and Lucinia's, and there was never any question in her mind that she would share fully in their upbringing and their education. Lucinia never seemed at all resentful of that partial usurpation, and no jealousy developed between the two sisters-in-law, who always seemed closer than many natural sisters. In fact, being both dark haired and dark-eyed, slender and graceful, they could easily have been mistaken for sisters. Catrianne was older by more than a year, but the difference was not obvious and Catrianne never attempted to claim any kind of seniority, always accepting meekly that Lucinia, as Alastor's wife, was the mistress of the house.

Alastor and Lucinia's first child was born on the first Monday after New Year's Day, which is known throughout Christendom as Handsel Monday. A handsel is a gift made to celebrate a new beginning, as a coin might be placed in the pocket of a freshly-tailored coat. Alastor felt that his son could be seen as exactly such a gift, bestowed upon his marriage, and he was determined to make the most of him.

"Might we call him Handsel, do you think?" Alastor asked Lucinia and Catrianne.

"It is a good name," they both said. Although Catrianne necessarily left the ultimate decision to Lucinia, there was never any possibility that she might deviate from such a unanimously approved opinion.

Every choice that is made in human life affects the range of further choices, and when the second child was due to be born Alastor said to Lucinia and Catrianne: "If our second-born is a girl, we ought not to call her Gretel."

Lucinia had never considered that as a possibility, so ruling the name out coast her nothing, but she was curious as to Alastor's reasons for making the remark, so she asked: "Why not?"

"Because I remember a tale that Catrianne's nurse used to tell me when I was a small boy, in which two children named Handsel and Gretel are abandoned in the wild forest by their father, a poor woodcutter, at the behest of their uncaring step-mother. The old crones who lived in the vicinity of my father's foundry loved tales of that sort, and the nurse to whom my father was obliged to confide Catrianne after my mother's death seemed to know hundreds of them. She used to delight in telling them, while she served the functions of my governess as well as Catrianne's nurse."

"I was too young to pay close attention to then when she told them to my brother," Catrianne explained, "but Alastor was at a very suggestive age, and some of the tales made a deep impression on him. I know that one, which is common even in the town, but it never frightened me in the way it seemed to have frightened Alastor. Not that it matters: who would want to call a child Gretel anyway?"

"It's precisely because the tale is common, even in the town," Alastor said, "that many people might think that Handsel and Gretel make a natural pair, and having already called one child Handsel, might think it quite appropriate to call a second Gretel—but there are omens in tales, and I do not think the example of that one ought to be followed. The lost children are captured and tormented by an evil fay, and although the tale ends happily enough for them—as all tales are bound by the principles of storytelling to do—I think that it might be dangerous to tempt fate in that fashion."

"You're not a woodcutter, my dear," Catrianne replied. "Our maternal grandfather was, according to father, but he died before either of us was born, and we live in the town now. We left the wild forest behind us when we left the highlands, and although I often miss the days when you and I used to roam there, I'm not sure at all that we ought to carry its legacy of sinister beliefs with us."

Lucinia, however, agreed entirely with Alastor that there really were omens and hidden meanings in ancient tales—of which she had an abundant supply of her own, which she had heard in early childhood—and that it was necessary to be very careful in naming children.

Catrianne shrugged her shoulders. "No matter," she said, again. "Ruling out one name still leaves thousands from which to choose—unless you deem that the supposed wisdom of old crones sets others out of bounds, for any of the ominous reasons of which old crones always seem to have an abundant supply."

"You should not be so dismissive of what our father calls superstitions," Alastor said, pensively. "Father would have no truck with any such convictions, and frequently got angry if anyone tried to tell him that there was a kernel of truth in the old tales of the fae-folk that the forest-dwellers loved so much, but I have always suspected that there is real wisdom in that legacy, even though it is no longer easy to decipher. We may be far away now from what were once reputed to be the haunts of the fae-folk, in terms of the society we inhabit, but we are highlanders still. If we were still resident in the vicinity of the foundry, rumors would probably still be circulating to the effect that our mother was a changeling, and the crones might only have had to glance at you and Lucinia to begin whispering among themselves that both of you have the look of fays about you."

"Might you have been a changeling too, then?" Catrianne asked Lucinia. "Or were the same things said of your mother that were said of ours?"

"I am certainly no changeling," Lucinia replied, with perfect seriousness, "and nor was my mother. That did not prevent rumors being spread among our own community concerning her, though, and she was subjected to ostracism by her own folk for a long time, on the basis of a suspicion spread in whispers, so I understand what Alastor means. Fortunately, as you say, my sister, we live in the town now, and there is every chance that our children will be spared that kind of curse. Even so, we should be careful in naming them…and we must take care that they hear all the stories we know, when they are of an age to listen, for whatever their guidance might be worth."

"Here in the town," said Catrianne, "it's often said that children must make their way in the real world, and that stories of the fae-folk will only fill their heads with silly ideas and unreasonable expectations."

"Some people do say that," admitted Alastor, "but the town-dwellers have merely devised a new armory of stories, which seem to them to be more appropriate to the order and discipline of urban life. For myself, I would rather our children heard some of those that I heard in my early childhood, which I loved so much, and any that Lucinia treasures in the same way—for they are, after all, our flesh and blood."

"What name did you have in mind for your second child, then?"

Catrianne asked him.

"In spite of my experience with my own father, I cannot help thinking, or at least hoping, that our son will choose to follow me in working wood with his hands," Alastor said. "I would like him to master the grain of the wood, in order that he might make pipes, harps, fiddles and lutes. In the same way, I would like to hope that our daughter might complement Handsel's achievements with musical abilities, either by playing like you or possessing a singing voice the equal of her mother's. Let us give her a name that would suit a player or a songstress."

"Ever since she arrived here," said Catrianne, "Lucinia has been nicknamed Nightingale, although she has always insisted that the name would be more fittingly attributed to me—but if you mean what you say about the wisdom of stories, we ought not wish that name upon our daughter."

"Certainly not," Alastor agreed. "Another of the stories that our old nurse used to tell me, while I watched her rock you in your crib, sent the worst shivers down my spine. It was a tale of a little girl who fell into the care of a wicked man who knew the secret of training nightingales to sing by day, and who trained her to be a human nightingale of sorts. Even today, I shudder when I think of it."

"I know that story too," agreed Lucinia, "and I also know one about a nightingale that impaled itself on a thorn in order to stain a white rose red for a student who wanted to make a present of it to a girl, who then spurned it, so that the nightingale suffered for nothing. No, we certainly should not call our daughter, if the child I am carrying turns out to be a daughter, Nightingale…or any name with a similar meaning."

"The little girl in the story Catrianne's nurse used to tell me was imprisoned in a cage by a prince, was she not?" said Alastor. "She was set to sing in the depths of the wild forest, but suffered misfortune enough to break her heart, and she refused to sing again, until she fell into the clutches of her former master, who…."

"Please don't," begged Lucinia. "Your memory is good, but that story has always haunted me, too, for very particular reasons."

"You know, then," Alastor deduced, "that your name means 'nightingale' in Latin? But I thought your people spoke a different language, and had only learned ours after settling in the high forest? I had assumed that the similarity was a coincidence."

Lucinia did not have to answer that, because Catrianne interrupted. "Never mind that," she said to Alastor. "I want to know how the story ends," she said. "What did the little girl's master do? I was too young to listen when my nurse first told you the stories, and although she repeated many of her favorite tales to me when I grew old enough to pay attention,

I don't remember that one."

Not wanting to cause his wife the slightest distress, however, Alastor, was quick to change the subject, or at least to return to the real subject of the discussion. "I wonder if we might call our daughter—if, as you say, the child you are carrying should turn out to be a daughter—Chanterelle, after the E string of a musical instrument: the one to which the melody is usually sung? That way, it would suit her whether she showed a talent for playing or for singing."

"But the word has other meanings, does it not?" asked Catrianne, dubiously. "A chanterelle is also a kind of mushroom—a highly-prized edible mushroom, to be sure, but still, a mushroom is a mushroom."

"Oh," said Lucinia, "but it's such a beautiful name. I love it. Yes, my darling, if our second child is a girl, I would love her to be called Chanterelle."

"Chanterelle is an excellent choice, then," said Catrianne, obligingly. "At least no one ever heard a story about a little girl named Chanterelle, so far as I know. But what if the baby turns out to be a boy?"

The discussion continued, but there is no need to record the rest of it here, for the child was indeed a girl, and she was named Chanterelle.

II

The Secret Stories

As soon as Handsel and Chanterelle were old enough to hear stories, Alastor, Lucinia and Catrianne were careful to tell them the tales that that they thought appropriate for them to hear. They told them tales that were popular in the town as well as those they remembered from their own childhoods in the highlands, but they had a natural preference for the highland tales, which Alastor and Lucinia remembered with an acute nostalgia, and in which Catrianne too found a special pleasure.

Each of them often told tales while they were alone with one or other of the children, but it was by no means uncommon for tales to be told while all five of them were together, with the adults taking turns to serve as storyteller. On such occasions, hearing the tales told again, in the company of the children, added an extra pleasure to the remembrance of their own childhood stirred up within them. The tales, and their telling, acquired a new significance in that context, and a further charm.

In the course of those gatherings, when Alastor, Lucinia and Catrianne took turns to serve as narrator, it soon became obvious that although Lucinia knew many of the same stories as Alastor and Catrianne, as well as some that they did not know—just as they knew some that she had never heard—the versions she had been told as a child were often different in detail, and in attitude from the versions known to Catrianne's nurse.

Almost all of the stories known to all three of them featured fays, as the principal species of the fae-folk were usually known in the tales, and almost all of them assumed that there were fays who treated humans benevolently and others that treated them malevolently, but Lucinia's versions sometimes attributed different and more elaborate motivations to the fays of either kind. Catrianne noticed, however, that when Lucinia repeated stories that she or Alastor had previously told, her narrations often fell into line with theirs, or at least came to resemble them more closely, as if she were giving their versions preference to her own, at least while all of them were together.

When Catrianne mentioned that to Alastor, he said: "I suppose that she doesn't want the children to be confused by hearing different versions of the stories, and as you and I are two and she is only one, it seems more convenient to adapt her versions to mirror ours."

"Isn't it odd, thought," Catrianne remarked, "that there should be different versions of the same tales?"

"Not really," said Alastor. "Tales vary a good deal from place to place and between the town and the city, and individual tellers are always changing them at their own whim. You have to remember that although you and Lucinia are both highlanders, and both children of the forest, her people seem to have been relatively recent settlers, whose ancestors were nomads. Between themselves, they still speak a language that bears no resemblance to ours, although they have all learned ours in order to communicate with us. It's quite natural that the versions of the tales that Lucinia was told as a child differ from those your old nurse told us—in fact, the surprising thing is that she knows so many of the same ones. Tales do travel across all kinds of frontiers, though, storytellers always being avid to adopt and adapt the bare bones of them to their own way of thinking. The ones we know probably have widely scattered points of origin, and have become somewhat confused during the process of transmission."

That all made such perfect sense that Catrianne accepted it wholeheartedly, and there was absolutely no malice intended in the casual remark she then made.

"Well, I suppose she adapts her versions to mirror ours when we're listening, but as their mother, she's alone with them more frequently than you or me; perhaps she tells them her own versions then."

"But that would defeat the object of the mimicry," Alastor pointed out.

Catrianne frowned slightly on discovering that she had said something silly, and sought for something to say that might repair, or at least at cover up, her error. "Well, she might tell them secret stories, which she considers unsuitable for our more civilized ears."

"Perhaps she does," said Alastor, laughing. "I confess that when I'm alone with one or both of the children, I often whisper confidences to them that I would hesitate to voice to you or Lucinia. Perhaps you do the same. Chanterelle is a particularly good listener, don't you find, and very discreet, given that she lags a little behind Handsel's understanding?"

"Do you think so?" asked Catrianne, laughing in her turn. "I sometimes think her more subtle and more complicated than her brother—and she's a girl, of course, which means that she is naturally cleverer and more skilled in dissimulation."

"What a strange thing to say," said Alastor. "What need do you have to dissimulate, who have no husband from whom to keep necessary secrets? Surely you have nothing you need to hide from a brother who has had you full confidence since you first learned to talk?"

"Do you think so?" she replied, and then added: "Well, perhaps you're right," in a tone that might have suggested the opposite to anyone but Alastor—who, having always been less subtle and less complicated than his sister, was always more inclined to take things at face value.

Alastor did notice, however, that both of his children loved stories featuring the fae-folk far more than stories that only had human characters. He was not sure whether to attribute that to the reflection of the storytellers' own fondness and preference, or whether there was something intrinsic to the stories that struck a chord in their infantile souls. Their own preferences were not identical, of course, but Alastor thought it only to be expected at his son would be particularly attracted to tales of adventure and derring-do, in which the heroic deeds of princes, knights or other heroes were placed in the foreground, while Chanterelle liked quieter and more mysterious tales—although not necessarily those in which princesses or goose-girls took center stage.

Handsel, as might be expected, given his name, was particularly fond of the tale of Handsel and Gretel, and Alastor tried to adapt it further for his taste by giving Handsel credit for both initiative and activity in extracting the captured children from the lair of the evil fay. Handsel also liked tales with an Oriental flavor, and tales derived from chivalric romance, which routinely featured heroes confronted with strange and dangerous circumstances, from which they had to extract themselves by means of a combination of ingenuity and swordplay.

Chanterelle, on the other hand, seemed to have a particular liking for a tale of a bronze-founder who was lured away from his family by a fay who had fallen in love with him, until he was eventually recalled to his duty by the tolling of a church bell he had made, which had fallen into a lake but continued to toll mysteriously in its depths. Catrianne had initially told the children that story to help them understand the kind of work her father did, although the bell was made of bronze rather than iron and she assured them that Ernand was not at all the kind of man to be seduced by a fay. Chanterelle also liked tales set in the forest, where her other grandfather had lived—although Lucinia tended to be rather vague about exactly what he had done there, except for resisting strongly the suspicion that he might have been a woodcutter or charcoal-burner.

"My mother," she said, firmly, if pressed on the point, "would never have harmed a tree."

"But your mother is not your father," Catrianne observed, "and men often have ideas different from their wives."

"Alastor and I do not," Lucinia insisted, although that was not the issue on which slight suspicion had been cast. "Alastor loves trees as much as I do."

"Which doesn't prevent him from dissecting their living flesh in order to make musical instruments," Catrianne riposted, always inclined, when she sensed an argument, to try to win it, even though nothing was further from her mind than hurting anyone's feelings by so doing.

"In fact, that's not entirely true," Alastor was quick to put in. "Trees are not like humans, who only have a few dead parts in association with their quick—hair, nails and the outermost layer of the skin—and seem to die all at once. Trees are much slower to die, and the parts of the living tree that are akin to the quick of our own flesh consist of the layer immediately below the bark, and the heartwood. Most of the other layers of the xylem are dead long before the tree itself dies, no more alive than your hair or your fingernails, and it's those layers—the death within the life—that provide the raw material for workmanship."

"That's not the point," Lucinia put in. "Trees accept being carved, for certain purposes, and one of those is the making of music. The forest used to love music. The forest was always willing to make the sacrifice of individual trees for certain purposes, of which music was one. Even now...."

But there she stopped, in confusion, as if she feared that she might already have said more than she intended, and more than she would have wished, if she had not been carried away.

"Does the forest no longer love music, then?" asked Catrianne, having observed Lucinia's use of the past tense. "Does it no longer make sacrifices?"

Lucinia did not answer, and Alastor, perceiving that she might appreciate a little moral support, intervened. "Forest folk—genuine forest folk—don't have the same attitude to the forest as we do," he attempted to explain. "They're far closer to nature than people like our father, who lived surrounded by the forest, but in a clearing contrived amid quarries and mines, as far from the forest spiritually as it's possible to be. You and I, as children loved the forest and loved to spend time there, but we always went into it as invaders, from another world. For Lucinia's mother and her family, it was quite different. We see the forest as something static and unchanging, but they have a sense of its antiquity, its transformations. You can glimpse that in some of Lucinia's stories as well as turns of phrase that sound odd to us. Then again, her ancestors came from elsewhere, and might well have handed down memories and stories about different forests."

"I can understand that," Catrianne agreed, "but it's all rather vague.

How much do you really know about her ancestors?" She turned to Lucinia to add: "How much do you?"

Lucinia still showed no inclination to say any more.

"I met her mother," Alastor said, defensively, although it hardly constituted an answer to Catrianne's question.

"But not her father?"

"No," Alastor admitted. "He was long dead, I think. She and her mother lived alone."

Catrianne looked at Lucinia then, with an interrogative gaze that was impossible to ignore. "That's true," Lucinia said. "When I met Alastor, I was living in the forest with my mother...almost alone."

"Almost?"

"My mother had a sister, Amanita, who lived nearby and visited us frequently, even when the rest of the community shunned us, but she and my mother were...estranged...like you and your father."

"I see," said Catrianne. "So you never actually knew your father, then, any more than I knew my mother? Do you have any memory of him at all?"

"No, none."

Catrianne nodded at that, implying that she understood that perfectly, because it corresponded with her own experience of her absent mother, although it seemed only natural for her to ask, in consequence: "And were you estranged from your mother in the same way that I have become estranged from my father? Is that why she didn't come to your wedding, and never comes to visit you?"

Alastor's father had not come to his wedding, and had never come to visit him, and although Alastor still called at the foundry when he happened to pass it while traveling on business, Catrianne had not been back there since she had left to join Alastor in the town.

Lucinia hesitated, but eventually said: "My mother and I love one another very dearly...but yes, we're...estranged now, in a way. I don't think it will ever be possible for us to see one another again."

Catrianne wanted to ask more questions, but Alastor put his hand on her arm and warned her with his gaze to desist. It was evidently a sore point. Naturally, she did desist, for the time being. That was only one of several issues about which she had effectively been forbidden to talk, however, and about which her curiosity was sharpened by the continual prohibitions. She continued to raise them occasionally, as subtly and as slyly as she could, always hoping to obtain more information in order to sate her natural curiosity.

Another such question was the story of the little girl whose wicked guardian knew the secret of making nightingales sing by day. Catrianne knew that both Alastor and Lucinia knew the story, although neither of them wanted to tell it, even to her, let alone to their children.

"They're too young," Alastor told his sister, when she once suggested, pointedly, when all five of them were present, that he tell it, hoping to rally the children's pleading to her support.

"But Handsel and Chanterelle must both be much older now than you were when my old nurse told it to you, over my cradle," Catrianne argued. Handsel was then six years old, and Chanterelle five.

"Yes, but it was too horrible at that age," Alastor said.

"Alastor's right," said Lucinia supportively.

"But stories have to prepare them for the fact that life has its horrors," Catrianne argued. "You love telling them the tale of Handsel and Gretel, and they love hearing it, even though it's about two children abandoned and left for dead by their parents, which must surely be an ultimate horror, from their viewpoint. And the story abut the bell-founder that I tell them, simply because it has a founder it, is also about a man who deserts his family, whose wife and children don't even know what has become of him—in much the same way that I didn't know what had become of you when you got lost in the mountains and found, or were found by, Lucinia and her mother. That was quite horrible, I can assure you."

"I'm sorry," Alastor said. "I didn't mean to desert you. It was an accident. I was hurt when my horse threw me. I couldn't walk properly for several days."

"I know. That's not the point. How old were you when you first heard the story, Lucinia?"

"I can't remember, exactly," Lucinia told her, evasively. "Too young, that's for sure. I understand what you're saying about having to prepare children for bad things, but…."

She left it there.

"But the real reason that neither of you wants to tell the story," Catrianne objected, "can't have anything to do with the age of her children, because you don't want to tell it to me either, which you could easily do when we're alone, without telling them."

"That's true," Alastor admitted, "but I can't tell stories about nightingales without thinking about Lucinia and you, who have been so frequently likened to nightingales. And because of that, I can't even think about the story without shuddering. That's why I don't want to tell it, even to you, in private."

"You're too squeamish by half," Catrianne told him, although she was careful to say it in a tone that suggested that she did not intend to scold him. "And what's your excuse?" she asked Lucinia.

"I'll tell it to you if you insist," Lucinia said, quietly, "in secret. But once you've heard it, you'll know it, and you'll never be able to get the image out of your mind. You're my sister; I love you too much to want to hurt you, and it's a story that hurts."

Catrianne was slightly taken aback by that, and once again refrained from insisting, for the time being. She did want to have the last word, though. "In actual fact," she said, using a phrase the commonplace in the town, although rarely applied to actual facts—"nightingales aren't very good singers at all. It's the mere fact of their singing by night that's remarkable, not the quality of their performance."

"Why can't we hear them?" Handsel put in, then, in his naïve fashion. "I hear birds singing early in the morning, but I've never heard any bird singing at night."

"Owls hoot and screech by night." Alastor put in, "but I don't suppose you can call that singing."

"There aren't any nightingales in the town," Catrianne told her nephew. "They're rare even in the forest around the foundry, where I was spent my childhood."

"As rare as the fae-folk?" asked Chanterelle.

"Not quite that rare," Catrianne admitted. "I've heard nightingales, I've but never seen a fay."

"Have you, Mother?" Handsel asked.

"Heard nightingales? Oh, yes. But your Aunt Catrianne is right. Their twittering is pretty enough, but they're not the best singers among the forest birds."

"And fays?" asked Chanterelle. "Have you seen fays?"

But Lucinia did not reply to that question.

As usual, in such circumstances, Alastor intervened. "Did you know that your mother's name means nightingale, in Latin?" he said. "I think that's part of the reason why the neighbors gave her the nickname."

"But Catrianne is the one who plays the flute," Lucinia put in, "which sounds more like birdsong than my voice. And her name, according to Zebedee, comes from the Greek *katharos*, which means purity."

Zebedee was no longer working with his hands, and Alastor had long since qualified for his mastery, but he still maintained a warm relationship with the old man, whom he and all his family regarded as a fount of wisdom—and, indeed, Zebedee had once been to school, and owned a number of printed books. Alastor had become an enthusiastic reader himself, and so had Catrianne, but they knew that the books the old man owned, and was only too pleased to lend them, were only a tiny fraction of those he had read in his lifetime, even though printed books had been exceedingly rare in his youth. Strangely enough, Lucinia also showed glimpses of learning that could only have come from books, and admitted, if questioned, that her mother had learned to read long ago, and had delighted in reading any books that she or her sister Amanita had been able to acquire.

"If Catrianne means purity, it's by no means an inappropriate name for you, my sister," Alastor observed, "although I doubt that's why my parents chose it, knowing no Greek. In the same language, Zebedee says, my name means avenger, but that doesn't fit me at all. I'm a very placid person."

"What does my name mean?" Handsel asked.

"And mine?" asked Chanterelle.

The appropriate explanations had to be given, at length.

The eventual result of those adroit changes of subject was not only that Catrianne did not get too hear the full story of the man who knew the secret of getting nightingales to sing by day, but that Chanterelle did not get to find out whether her mother hand ever seen a fay…unless Lucinia told her the answer in secret, in the same way that she had promised, reluctantly, to tell her the story.

III

Zebedee and the Children

As Alastor had hoped, Handsel soon showed an interest in wood-work, and he was soon allowed to go with his father to Zebedee's work-shop—although Zebedee no longer worked there now—while his father devoted himself to his daily labors. Alastor gave him pieces of wood to whittle and old Zebedee showed him how to hold a knife in such a way as to avoid cutting himself, and supervised the boy's efforts as best he could—although cuts inevitably followed, and floods of tears, and bandages, and remonstrations aimed at Alastor and Handsel alike by both Lucinia and Catrianne.

Handsel showed an aptitude for music too, and that led to fewer remonstrations. Alastor gave him instruments of various kinds to play with, and showed him how to place his fingers in such a way as to produce different notes when he blew into them or plucked their strings. The boy was soon able to produce tunes of a sort on various instruments, ranging from simple whistles or the sets of seven tubes that were generally called panpipes, to lyres and lutes. It was at that point that Catrianne took over that aspect of his education, and began to teach him to produce more complicated tunes, including those that she had learned from Lucinia.

If Catrianne had wanted to take over the boy's instruction entirely, though, she was soon disappointed. He persisted in returning to his father's workshop and picking up knives, and soon learned to do so without cutting his fingers. He thus learned to produce, if not viable musical instruments, at least small sculptures in wood that had a certain artistry, which drew an admiration from his parents, his mother and his aunt that was not as exaggerated by kindness as might have been necessary had his fingers been less adept.

Gradually, Handsel's play turned into a genuine apprenticeship, which pleased his father enormously, although his skills as a player of music only developed in a limited fashion under Catrianne's tutelage. The logic of the situation, which compelled Handsel to spend the bulk of his time with his father and his aunt, inevitably left Chanterelle in her mother's company for long hours. Handsel and Chanterelle loved one another dearly, but the pattern of life gradually drew them apart, except in the evenings, long in winter, when the whole family gathered together, initially for storytelling and for Lucinia to sing to Catrianne's accompaniment, but increasingly, as time went by, for more complex performances in which both children became involved as their abilities permitted and their further training required.

Chanterelle was certainly not a disappointment either; she proved to have a lovely voice. She sang by day and she sang by night, alone or in the company of her family. On Sundays she and her mother both sang in the choir at the church which Alastor, Lucinia and Catrianne attended regularly, not because any of them was particularly devout, but because it was the kind of thing that respectable townsfolk did. It was necessary for them to be respectable, not simply for the sake of Alastor's good reputation but for the sake of living comfortably with their neighbors, none of whom was particularly devout either, but all of whom had opinionated standards of decency that they were keen to uphold. Lucinia and Chanterelle's collaboration in the singing of hymns seemed to the congregation, for reasons they could not quite understand, to be a very model of decency.

As dutiful parents, Alastor and Lucinia made some attempt to teach Chanterelle the arts of needlework, but Lucinia had never had any more enthusiasm for them than Catrianne, regarding sewing and darning as the most taxing of household chores, and she was not at all disappointed when Chanterelle showed the same antipathy, as if it ran in her blood. By way of compensation, however, Catrianne had cultivated a certain skill in knitting with wooden needles, and had taught Lucinia the art in question; both of them hoped that Chanterelle might eventually take that up, when her hands became less clumsy.

Certain other aspects of the children's education were entrusted to old Zebedee, who had become a substitute father to Alastor, and who adored his children—and, indeed, his wife and sister. It was Zebedee who taught the children to read and write, and also to calculate. He took great delight in so doing, and told Alastor that, since he was no longer able to do anything useful with his arthritic hands, it was a great relief to him to have found another purpose with which to lend meaning to his final years. When his housekeeper died, he began to take his evening meals at Alastor's house, which was situated not far from the workshop, above which he slept, and he was always a welcome guest.

Having lived all his life in the town, Zebedee knew the stories that were popular there, but had never heard many of those that Alastor,

Catrianne and Lucinia had told their children, and which their children obligingly related to their "grandfather." They stirred his own curiosity, and he began to ask Alastor and Catrianne questions about the folk in whose neighborhood they had lived, and to ask Lucinia about her own people—questions that soon revealed that Alastor and Catrianne knew less than they had always assumed, revealing areas of ignorance to which they had never previously given any thought.

Catrianne asked Zebedee once, in secret, whether he knew the tale about the little girl and the man who had the secret of teaching nightingales to sing by day.

"No," he told her, "but I do know that tales about nightingales are almost always incorrect in their natural history, like the nickname that our neighbors have given Lucinia—and, for that matter, her own name, if it is not by pure coincidence that it resembles the Latin word for nightingale. It is, in fact, male nightingales that sing, not female ones."

"Really?" asked Catrianne, who had always assumed the opposite, as the stories tended to do.

"So I believe," Zebedee told her. "Although, in fairness, I ought to say that it is not unknown for scholars to be proved wrong and folk-wisdom to be proved right, so I dare not insist. And although I do not know the ending of the story about which you asked me, I do know what scholars believe to be the secret of making nightingales sing by day."

And he told her that secret, which allowed Catrianne to deduce the end of the story, and to understand why it had made Alastor and Lucinia shiver with horror.

But at least Lucinia is wrong, she thought, *and I am no more entitled to be reckoned a nightingale than she is, for we are both female, and if Zebedee's scholar are right, it is the male birds that sing. It is a nickname whose ominous connotations I can reject in full confidence.*

It was not a subject that she ever brought up again with her brother and sister-in-law, and in their family gatherings, the interrogations to which the family subjected old Zebedee were invariably restricted to less unsavory aspects of his scholarship, such as the history of the town where he had always lived.

"When I was a boy," he told them, "It was little more than a village. Since then it has grown so considerably that it will soon be a city, and would already be reckoned one if its people had ever taken the trouble to build a cathedral—but they have never been very devout. Its inhabitants were more enthusiastic in those days to build good walls than better churches—an enthusiasm that testifies to an admirable practicality. Invading armies had rarely passed this way in my forefathers' times, but once the road connecting the town to the port was paved for heavy vehicles, it also became far more convenient for military transportation, and once bronze cannon, virtually unknown even in my father's day, became commonplace in their employment in neighboring territories, the town council immediately began to think that the town needed sturdy and powerful defenses. That is why you see it as it is today, with thick walls, heavy gates and steep ramparts."

"The transformation gave my father a lot of work," Alastor observed. "He told me once that there had been a time when his own father was principally occupied in making church bells in bronze, and occasional iron plowshares, but that demand had shifted markedly toward cannon and all manner or iron weapons and iron armor to defend against it. He sometimes said that he wished he had become a swordsmith, but that that was highly specialized work, as much because of the ornamentation of the weapons that gentlemen like to carry as what he used to call the 'honest iron' of their blades. He admitted, though, that the demand for plowshares and horseshoes had also increased dramatically as the town expanded, because urban populations need more surrounding farmland to feed their population, which inevitably increases the distance over which crops have to be transported to market."

"Alas," said Zebedee, "I think there are very few swords that can count as 'honest iron,' and no cannon at all. Nor am I entirely certain about bells, for all their utility in timekeeping and sounding alarms. Plowshares, on the other hand…there's veritable honesty. Tilling the soil is the true work of human beings, and agriculture the true sustenance of civilization."

When he said that, however, he noticed Lucinia drawing Chanterelle closer to her, and putting her arms around her as if to shield her from something dangerous, or at least improper."

"You don't agree, my dear?" he said, slightly puzzled.

"On the contrary," she replied, mildly. "I agree entirely that agriculture is the true sustenance of civilization, and the horse-drawn plow its mainstay."

"But you don't entirely approve," observed the old woodworker, shrewdly. "You were born and bred in the high forest, and descended from nomads who doubtless kept some sort of livestock but never manipulated plows. You don't like civilization…even though you're enjoying all its benefits now."

"I like it well enough," Lucinia conceded, reluctantly, "and anyway, the forest is dying. Civilization is the future."

"According to my father," Alastor murmured, "iron is the future."

"But you agree with your lovely wife," Zebedee said, "as a loyal husband should. You're both nostalgic for the past, even though you can see where the world is going, and accept it. But you needn't worry over-much. The forests will always be there, including the one surrounding Ernand's foundry. Civilization will always need wood as well as iron, for fuel and materials. Metals have a role to play in making music, and not just for military signals and fanfares, but there's an affinity between wood and music of which you're very keenly aware. The forest will never be allowed to die. Quite the reverse: it will be very carefully conserved."

But he saw tears then, trickling from Lucinia's eyes, and she was holding Chanterelle even more tightly than before, as if she were trying desperately to protect her from something, even though she knew that the gesture was futile. "You don't agree, my dear?" the old man said, disconcerted, because the last thing he would have wanted to do was upset his "little Nightingale."

"It's nothing," Lucinia said, plainly lying.

"Lucinia misses the forest," Alastor intervened, trying to cover for his wife, as always. "We all do, of course—Catrianne and I spent so much time there when we were children, escaping from the noise and heat of the foundry—but Lucinia had never known anything else until I took her away, abruptly and permanently."

"Why permanently?" asked Zebedee. "You had to come to the town, of course, to serve your apprenticeship with me, but you're a master now, and you have an established reputation. It's said for several leagues around that there's a veritable magic in the way you work with wood, and that the musical instruments you construct are unparalleled in the sweetness of their sound—which is true. There's no reason any more for you to cling to my old workshop. You could build one of your own, and live anywhere along the road you like. Since you all love the forest so much, why not go to live closer to its heart?"

Alastor was about to say that that might be a good idea, although it would feel like a kind of desertion to leave Zebedee's workshop—by which he really meant Zebedee himself—but it was Lucinia's turn to interrupt.

"No," she said, simply. "I couldn't bear that. It's better to stay in the town, until the children are grown."

Her voice was so distraught that Zebedee was not the only one who wanted to say "But why not?" but did not dare to do so, lest it add to her distress.

Handsel, however, was not yet at an age to be as diplomatic as his elders.

"I'd like it," he said, firmly. "I've heard so much about the forest, in tales and everyone's memories, but I've only been outside the town walls for short rides. I've seen the forest from the ramparts, but I've never been there. I'd like to live there."

"Me too," said Chanterelle.

Lucinia hugged her even closer. "Perhaps you would, and perhaps you will one day—I hope so," she told her son and daughter. "But it's dangerous—even more dangerous now than it was in olden days, and the tales don't lie about how dangerous it was, even then—and we need to wait until you're older."

"Because of the bears and the wolves?" suggested Handsel.

Lucinia hesitated before saying: "Yes."

Handsel might have let it go at that, but Zebedee had noticed the hesitation, and his curiosity had been stirred again.

"What else?" he said.

Again, Lucinia hesitated before saying; "There are poisonous things there."

"That's true," said Catrianne, supportively. "Alastor and I used to pick mushrooms and berries in the season, but we had to be very careful, especially with the mushrooms, to have them approved by an adult before eating them. We learned to pick out the best ones, though—the chanterelles." She glanced at her niece and smiled.

"And there are other plants, which you only have to touch in order to come out in a painful rash," Alastor put in. "Do you remember, Cat, what a painful time we had learning that!"

"But it didn't stop you, did it?" Zebedee observed.

"Children are reckless," Alastor sighed. "That's why we try so hard to protect our own, so that they don't have to learn the hard way. And Cat and I were escaping from the Foundry, which was far worse. Here, Handsel and Chanterelle have a haven of security, where everyone loves them and they're happy. But even so, we ought to hire a trap one day and go for an excursion, to show them the forest."

"You can show them the trees," Lucinia murmured, still emotional, "but you can't show them the forest."

"It's true," Zebedee conceded, "that people in general, especially townspeople, often have difficult seeing the wood for the trees. And people like me, who have spent our lives dealing with pieces of trees, fresh from the sawmill rather than the forest, often have difficulty even visualizing the tree."

"There are trees in the town, in gardens and avenues," Handsel said. "I know what a tree is. I can climb trees."

"I know what you mean, Zebedee," Alastor said, "but we still get a feel of the tree, don't we, you and I, when we work the wood? Perhaps even something beyond the tree. I know you feel, as I do, that there's always a right way and a wrong way to work a particular block of wood, with a lathe, a chisel or a knife, and that there's also a perfect way, which only masters like you and I can find: the way the wood wants and needs to be worked. And that doesn't come from the shape or the texture of the block…it's something deeper, more essential. The spirit of the tree…or perhaps even the forest. Not when merely turning ax-handles, or anything to hold iron, of course, but when making things that make music, as we love to do. The wood is dead, but it was once alive, and it retains something from that…a soul. It's a pity we never had the art of sculpting living wood, the way…."

He stopped.

"What do you mean?" Zebedee prompted.

"Sorry," said Alastor. "For a moment there I thought I remembered something. I did, in fact, but it was only something I dreamed…a grove of trees, with all kinds of unknown symbols sculpted in the living wood, so that they became books of a sort, recording ideas…and music…except that the language was foreign, and I couldn't understand it…but it was just a dream. I've had it more than once. It's strange, isn't it, how you can sometimes return in dreams to places you've visited in previous dreams, and which seem familiar because of it…."

"I often dream about the forest too," said Catrianne, "But I've never dreamed about trees sculpted with words and music, in any language."

"I dream about the forest too," Chanterelle put in. "And it is frightening, sometimes. But other times…it's wonderful."

"You've only ever heard tales of the forest, my love," said Catrianne. "Of course it seems wonderful, and sometimes frightening, because that's the way it is in tales."

"Not all of them…," said Chanterelle—but then stopped abruptly, as if she had almost said something that she was not supposed to say, and had only just stopped herself in time.

Lucinia was already hugging her tightly, but she clasped her head to her bosom, in such a way that the little girl's face disappeared from view, leaving nothing but a curtain of dark hair that was beginning to acquire the same silky gloss as her mother's and Catrianne's.

"Even I dream about forests sometimes," Zebedee supplied, "but that's not surprising. I've ridden through the forest many a time, in my youth, and even used to go hunting, once upon a time."

"Hunting bears?" Handsel immediately queried.

"No, not bears…or anything ferocious. We chased roe deer, but usually unsuccessfully. Deer are clever as well as nimble, and even with a good pack of hounds, they often got away. Why are you shuddering, my dear?"

The final question was addressed to Lucinia.

"Lucinia doesn't approve of hunting with dogs," Alastor explained. "I think she identifies with the deer rather than the hunters."

"So do I," said Catrianne. "I sometimes eat venison, but I have to avoid thinking about the way it's been killed. Roe deer are so beautiful. Wild pig I don't mind so much, or pheasants."

"Well, I hope you can forgive me, Nightingale, for the sins of my youth," said Zebedee. "I'm past all that now, quite harmless to any of God's creatures except chickens and the occasional trout…although my hands can hardly even handle a rod any more."

Lucinia did not show the slightest sympathetic reaction in favor of fish, or even domestic poultry.

"I'd like to go hunting," Handsel said. "It would be exciting."

"Especially if you run into a bear," said Alastor, "or a pack of wolves. Then you could be hunted yourself, and double the excitement."

"Please don't joke about things like that," said Lucinia.

"Too squeamish by half," muttered Catrianne, more to herself than to her sister-in-law. But she quickly added: "That's enough talk. Shall we make some music? We can all join in—a veritable orchestra."

Clearly, there had been enough talk for one evening, because the proposal was greeted with enthusiasm, and they did, indeed, all join in, although Zebedee's fingers were no longer able to handle any kind of instrument fluently, and Handsel still had to be reckoned inexpert—but Catrianne and Alastor played loudly and confidently, and Lucinia and Chanterelle sang beautifully, in perfect harmony.

Afterwards, Lucinia put Chanterelle to bed, while Handsel was allowed to stay up a little longer. It had long become standard practice not to send them to bed simultaneously, lest they keep one another awake with chatter and play. They shared the same room, for lack of any alternative, but they had beds on opposite sides, with their own curtains, and Handsel always went to sleep meekly enough if Chanterelle were already asleep, as she invariably was if Lucinia had put her to bed, because Lucinia had a knack to it that no one else could match. When asked how she did it, she always smiled and said: "It's a secret."

No one ever pressed her as to what the secret was, because nobody took the remark seriously, although she was sometimes overheard whispering to the child in a strangely musical fashion, incomprehensibly, perhaps in the unforgotten language of her own childhood, or perhaps in a private language that was theirs alone, invented for the purpose.

IV

The Story of the Forest

What Lucinia whispered to Chanterelle in order to put her to sleep was, in fact, their little secret. And the reason that it was incomprehensible to anyone else was that it consisted of stories told in a language that was partly inherited and partly improvised.

How had Lucinia taught her daughter to understand that language? That was a mystery—but it was a mystery that no one pursued, because anyone who overheard them whispering—Handsel most of all, but sometimes Alastor or Catrianne—simply assumed that Chanterelle did not understand it at all, and merely construed it as soothing sound, like birdsong.

In fact, though, Chanterelle did understand the terms of that language, even though she had no idea herself how she had learned them, and was unsure about many of their referents. It seemed to be in her blood, although Handsel was her brother, and he could not understand a word of it, so if it was hereditary, it had to be something passed down selectively from mother to daughter. In any case, it was definitely something special, between the mother and the daughter: a kind of harmony that they had, like the harmony they had when they sang together, and perhaps not unrelated to it. Perhaps Chanterelle learned the secret language by means of a kind of resonance, or perhaps it was a kind of magic, or both.

Either way, Chanterelle knew, at least to some extent, what the mysterious sounds signified. She understood. And she was glad to have a secret, because a secret can be a very precious thing, if carefully guarded, so carefully as to be protected from a father, a brother and an aunt, as well as everyone else.

So Chanterelle had the beginnings of an understanding of the language in which her mother whispered to her, and she understood a fraction, at least, of the stories that were told to her, little by little, in that language. She did not understand more than a tiny fraction, but she was accustomed to that. She had always been told stories of which she understood little or nothing at the first telling, but whose meaning filtered through gradually over time, until they became more comprehensible—not fully comprehensible, because there are so many stories that never do become fully comprehensible, even to their makers, let alone their tellers, but at least possessed of a superficial plausibility.

Even in her young mind—which was still very young indeed—Chanterelle had a suspicion that the meaning of the secret stories might take a long time to accumulate, and that full comprehension would always remain tantalizingly out of reach, but she did not mind that at all. For one thing, the stories had a music that made them pleasurable even while they remained largely incomprehensible, and for another, she was in no hurry at all to have them finished and complete, so that they would not require any further telling. She knew, somehow, that there was a limited supply, and that there would come a day, eventually, when there would be no more telling.

Because of that, perhaps she did not try as hard as she might have done, even with her immature mind, to understand the stories rapidly. She was more than content to take her time, to let them flow, without racking her brains as to what their exact significance might be, or why her mother was telling her secret stories at all.

Gradually, though, they accumulated, and there were three, in particular, that, although Chanterelle did not understand more than a tiny fraction of their implication, nevertheless came together with a coherency that was almost tangible, of which the one that seemed to be most important to her mother, and hence to her, although it was by far the most difficult to comprehend, was the story of the forest. That one Chanterelle was quite incapable of understanding—but her mother told it to her anyway, in fragments, repeatedly and insistently, intent on engraving its elements in her memory regardless of her incomprehension, in order that it would be there, in storage, for the day when comprehension might dawn in her evolving intellect.

This is the gist of that story, as the mother appeared to understand it, and appeared to organize it in her own far more flexible and subtle mind.

Once upon a time there had been a great forest. It was a truly vast forest, which extended all the way from an ocean now called the Atlantic in the west to a sea now called the Mediterranean in the south, and from the edge of cold steppes in the north and to bleak mountains in the east. The forest had various names in different parts of its extent, but the fays, who liked to think of themselves as the aristocracy of the fae-folk—somewhat to the resentment of the other species—called it Broceliande.

There had been a very early time when the forest was seamless and uninterrupted. It was home to many species of animals, including primitive humans, who had not yet mastered the use of fire then, and the fae-folk had been very primitive too, in their own way.

The forest was alive, not merely in the sense that the trees composing it were living beings, but in the sense that the entire forest constituted a collective entity, which had a mind of sorts. It was a mind incapable of self-conscious thought, but it was certainly not incapable of dreaming. Not that the forest was asleep, because the concept of sleep only makes sense by contrast with the concept of being awake, and the forest was neither awake nor asleep while it was perpetually dreaming.

The fae-folk were the figments of the forest's dream.

That does not mean that they were not real and substantial, but their reality and substance were not quite the same as the reality and substance of the animals of the forest, and the reality of the trees themselves. They were not immaterial, but their substance was a trifle mercurial, more prone to change than the duller matter of minerals, vegetables and animals. It was not that their substance was light, gaseous or ethereal, rather than solid, but rather as if it represented am additional state of matter, a state unique to the dream of the forest.

Some of the fae-folk were shapeshifters, prone to physical metamorphoses and sometimes able to provoke them. Most of them were magical to some degree, able to do things that animals and plants could not, but their powers were more limited than the tales that humans told, and even the tales they told one another, routinely took for granted. Fays, who had more conscious control of their magic than their kindred species, often possessed certain powers of fascination, the ability to generate light, and healing powers, but all those manifestations of the uncanny were more frequent and more sweeping when they occurred independently of the fays' will, at the whim of Broceliande's dream. Moreover, whenever a fay attempted to work magic by the power of her will, the success of her operation was dependent on the permission of the dream. Magical actions compliant with the whim of the dream were successful, sometimes in an exaggerated fashion, those contradictory to it failed, or even produced results opposite to those intended.

The unreliability of magic made fays wary of its employment, and also led some to take a particular interest in the magical art of dream-reading: the attempt to detect or intuit the whims of the dream with which magic ought to comply, and could not contradict without risk. Necessarily, however, dream-reading was subject to the same perversities as other kinds of magic; the whims of Broceliande could only be read with their own permission, and were sometimes liable to deceive. Because the dream was a dream, and not the product of conscious, rational thought, its whims were always unpredictable to some degree. Although the most ingenious dream-readers often felt that they had grasped some underlying logic or patterns to the whims of the dream, the anticipations provided by of their theses always failed eventually, more often sooner than later.

In the main, the magic accomplished by the dream, independently of the will, desires and prayers of its conscious figments, was much greater in its effects than the magic accomplished deliberately by those figments. The metamorphoses achieved by determination, even by fays, were often superficial, sometimes frustratingly temporary and sometimes awkwardly permanent, but those accomplished arbitrarily by the dream could be much more dramatic, involving changes in apparent dimension and mass, as well as form, far beyond those that even the most artful magician could operate by choice.

It was not surprising that humans, in trying to figure out the fae-folk on the basis of inadequate information and limited intelligence, made the mistake of thinking that they were always in control of the magic that happened around them, and that its effects were always consciously intended, because those fae-folk capable of conscious thought and a degree of rational calculation often made the same mistake themselves. When they changed shape, or the magic innate within them became manifest, especially when it did so in seemingly-consistent patterns, it was very difficult for them to think of it other than as something they had *done*, albeit without knowing exactly how or why. It was very tempting, and perhaps unavoidable, that they should think that there had to be a trick to the effects of the dream, of which they must be able to achieve mastery, if they could only figure out how.

Given that the conscious fae-folk thought that themselves, it was only natural for humans to jump to the same conclusion, and also to take the false deduction a step further, in convincing themselves that they too ought to be able to work magic if only they could figure out the trick to it, and master the requisite formula. They were wrong. Humans were not figments of Broceliande's dream, and they had no magic, although they sometimes became indirectly involved in it and entangled in its manifestations in the days when the forest was healthy, and even, occasionally, during the final phase of Broceliande's malady and agony.

Even had Broceliande been conscious, and capable of rational thought itself, it would not necessarily have followed that the forest could have controlled, directed or deliberately produced its own magic. After all, humans, some of whom eventually became conscious, and capable of a rudimentary simulacrum of rational thought, did not automatically acquire control over their dreams—and, in fact, found that control extremely elusive.

Perhaps there was an underlying logic and purpose to Broceliande's dreams, which was not immediately obvious to its figments, even to the fay dream-readers, let alone to its primitive human observers. On the other hand, perhaps not; logic might suggest that there ought to have been, and perhaps must have been, but the authority of logic to make such judgments has to be reckoned dubious in this instance.

At any rate, the conscious fae-folk had to live with the situation in which they found themselves: a situation both uncertain and tantalizing, which could be deeply frustrating for those among them who fancied themselves magiciennes, dream-readers or philosophers.

In truth, there were not many of fays who reckoned themselves philosophers. Philosophy is not entirely a human ailment, but humans tended to have a terrestrial near-monopoly even during the dotage of the forest, when Broceliande became moribund and the incentive for its figments to grapple mentally with that existential crisis became strong. Those fays who did become philosophers, as well as magiciennes and dream-readers, soon became keenly aware of the limitations and frustrations of their intellectual quest, especially those who thought themselves cursed with prophetic powers.

Humans who thought themselves possessed of prophetic powers sometimes considered them a blessing rather than a curse, but that only serves to confirm that they really were insane. Fays rarely made the same mistake—but that, alas, did not necessarily mean that they were perfectly sane.

While Broceliande was healthy, it seemed to the figments of its dream to be capable of enduring forever, and some of the fae-folk thought that of themselves, assuming that they were potentially capable of living forever, if they could avoid accidental or deliberate annihilation. When Broceliande ceased to be healthy, however, and began to die, its more intelligent figments accepted, albeit reluctantly, that the forest was not immortal, and that their days too were evidently numbered, perhaps as meanly as the days of mere tortoises or parrots. To make matters worse, the probability of their premature annihilation, not merely by violence but by virtue of new maladies to which they had never been subject before, increased dramatically.

It was a great humiliation, particularly to the fays, to discover that many of them were not only becoming as mortal as mere humans, but in many cases, even more fragile—although, by way of apparent compensation, some of them retained the ability to employ their magic to sustain more protracted lives and their powers of modest metamorphosis to retain the protracted appearance of youth.

The death of Broceliande did not seem to the figments of its dream to be a natural process. It seemed to them—or, at least, the great majority of them—to be a kind of murder, albeit an exceedingly slow murder: death by a trillion cuts.

In the beginning, the cuts had been trivial, mere scratches of which the forest could not have died. They were inflicted with flint and fragments of shell and bone. In themselves, they were trivial, but it was a beginning.

The more serious cuts were, however, those that inflicted much longer and deeper gashes in the body of the forest. That process began with paths, which humans made for the convenience of moving around in the forest. At one time, they began to claim, and perhaps to believe, that they had merely adopted existing animal trails, widening them and maintaining their clearance, but that was a myth. Animals do not make stable and enduring trails. Only human beings do that. So it was the humans, and only the humans, who, in making paths through the forest—not merely cutting it but beginning to slice and section it, to disrupt the continuity of its body—were culpable of its murder. It was human beings, and only humans, that many of the fae-folk thought it necessary to blame and hate for their own decline toward oblivion, for the inexorable extinction of the dream.

Again, had the matter stopped with footpaths, as well as flints, no fatal injury could have been inflicted, no irreparable damage done. But it did not stop, because humans were infected by the curse of "progress." Progress consisted of the increasing mastery of fire and the broadening of its applications. The forest had always been damaged occasionally by accidental fires, sometimes sustaining bad burns, but it had always recovered and regrown. With the aid of deliberate fires, though, humans were able to clear huge areas of forest, which did not regrow, because the land in question was claimed for a corollary invention of progress: the agriculture that, in collaboration with fire, produced the mainstay of human nutrition, bread. Sectors of forest were cleared in order to make land available for tillage. That was hard work, but humans were extremely laborious, and the wounds they inflicted on the forest in order to obtain farmland multiplied and extended inexorably.

Gradually, too, the implements that the humans used in order to torture and murder Broceliande improved. Flint was replaced, initially by bronze, and then, fatally, by the ultimate bane of Broceliande: iron. Paths, by degrees, became roads, dug with iron spades, filled with shards of rock produced by iron picks and tamped with iron presses: deep, wide cuts that extended for many miles, hacking the body of Broceliande to pieces.

The humans, of course, had no idea what they were doing. They could see the trees but they could not see the forest. They knew that the trees were alive, but not that they were part of a larger entity that was possessed of a more general, more mysterious, kind of life: a life capable of generating dreams, whose figments were the fae-folk.

Would they have cared if they had known?

Of course not.

The murder they committed was unwitting, but if they had known what they were doing they would have done it anyway, not even uncaringly, but gladly, viciously and sadistically. They were, after all, human. There was no absolution for them, in the eyes of the great majority of the fae-folk on the grounds that they did not know what they were doing, although there were a few exceptions to that general rule especially among the wiser fays.

In the epoch when Broceliande began to die, human beings did not know that Broceliande existed, but they did know that the fae-folk existed. In later eras, the scholars among them became doubtful about that—as well they might, since the fae-folk had almost ceased to exist by then—and also became doubtful that their ancestors had ever really known that they existed. Many of them, especially the philosophers who were beginning to appear in their midst in some profusion, like a kind of mental cancer, began to think that the fae-folk had only been the figments of a collective dream—which they had, although the human philosopher attributed the dream in question not to Broceliande's vast and fecund unconscious mind, but to the petty imagination of silly humans.

Like the fays, and with a similar lack of justification, humans were proud, not to say vainglorious.

It was, of course, ludicrous for human philosophers to think that the fae-folk might have been figments of their own shallow and shabby dreams, because human dreams have nothing to compare, even remotely, with the awesome creative power of Broceliande's dream, but it was an understandable mistake for philosophical members of a fundamentally narcissistic and egotistical species to make.

Sometimes, the rare philosophers among the fays suggested that humans were figments of the dream of some vast entity—perhaps the fever dream of the fluid iron that constituted the earth's hot core—but none of them every suspected for a minute that humans might be figments of the dreams of the fae-folk. That would have been monstrous as well as absurd.

Broceliande did not die all at once. Even human beings do not die all at once; individual cells within their bodies can continue living for days after the heart has stopped beating and all brain activity has ceased. In a sense, because Broceliande was made up of individual trees that were capable of independent life and of reproduction more-or-less indefinitely, even after the universal entity had perished, there was a sense in which fragments of Broceliande could continue to live a life of sorts, but as Broceliande itself was subjected to the torment and death of a trillion cuts, its mentality or its soul—the dreaming aspect of the whole—gradually shriveled and fragmented. Some of the remoter swathes of the great forest's sliced-up and multiply scarred body still retained a limited capacity for dreaming, and for sustaining figments of dream, including some kinds of fae-folk, but they were few, feeble and far between.

Even so, magic lived on, fugitively, and desperately, and those of the fae-folk who were self-conscious—most notably the fays—tried as best they could, in many and varied ways, to cope with the threat of impending extinction. Some were resigned, becoming reclusive and melancholy, simply waiting to die. Others were not, and decided to fight, to scheme, to formulate bold and sometimes bizarre plans for their survival. They were convinced that they had the means—magical means—if only they could contrive to bring those means under control. But that was easier thought than done: a conviction far easier to obtain psychologically than to put into action.

The few philosophers who existed among the fays hesitated between resignation and action, reluctant to settle for the former, in what seemed a cowardly fashion, but uncertain as to whether there was any point in attempting action unless and until they had a much better understanding of what action might be possible. In particular, they were preoccupied with the question of what the dream might be doing of its own accord, using them as its instruments, and whether there was anything they could do either to assist or subvert its intentions, if it had any intentions, and if they could figure out what those intentions might be.

Perhaps theirs was a hopeless task, but even some of those who suspected that it was utterly futile felt that they still had to try, that they still had to make an effort, and that even a futile effort might, in the end, be better than nothing, qualifying as heroism of a sort even in the face of certain defeat.

There was no substantial consensus among the surviving fays as to what they might attempt to do, or how they might prepare for any such attempt. Indeed, there were bitter arguments between them, which sometimes split families. But insofar as there was any common ground at all, it revolved around "the human question." If anything could be done to save some existential echo of Broceliande, the fay philosophers thought, some shard of the great forest's soul capable of staining a dream, it could not be done simply by ignoring humans and leaving them to continue their destructive work. Either human endeavor had to be stopped, or it had to be diverted or subverted in some way that would permit the survival of the dreaming entity, the survival of the dream, and hence the survival of at least some figments of the dream.

Humans were, of course, vulnerable to fays in various ways. Humans could be killed by fays as easily as by one another, but only in tiny numbers when increasingly rare opportunities cropped up. More significantly, however—at least in the eyes of many of the fays' would-be strategists—humans could be seduced and beguiled by fays; they could often be persuaded to do, or tricked into doing, what fays wanted them to do. The dream that was the true generator of the fays' magic was apparently very sympathetic, at least some of the time, to beguilement, and frequently granted abundant permission to attempts at seduction with the aid of glamour. All dream-readers observed that peculiarity of the dream's whim, although none could understand why it should be the case. In any case, the ability gifted to fays to seduce humans and persuade them to do what they wanted them to do was only useful if the fays could work out what humans might actually be able to achieve on their behalf; simple enough in trivial matters, that was much more difficult when it came to recruiting their assistance in opposing or easing the death of Broceliande.

There was, however, one side-effect of the fays' shapeshifting powers, with particular relevance to their propensity to take on forms capable of beguiling humans that their philosophers and strategists found intriguing. Although it was not invariably the case, fays that assumed human form sometimes did so to the extent that they could become pregnant by them and bear them children.

All fays were female. That was not the case with all of the fae-folk, but it was true of the fays, and was one of the aspects of their existence that led them to think of themselves as the natural aristocracy of the fae-folk, along with the corollary conviction that maleness was something essentially vulgar, if not positively disgusting. Some fays, at least, were capable of bearing children, but under what they considered to be normal circumstances, the children were always female. When the forest was healthy, that only happened rarely, because the fays were then capable of living indefinitely, and did not suffer accidental or violent death very often, thus not needing replenishment either by reproduction or by new figment-creation on the part of Broceliande.

When fays shifted shape to become near-perfect simulacra of human beings, however, they became capable of producing offspring with human husbands. In conformity with the principles of probability applicable to human matings, approximately fifty per cent of the offspring thus produced were female, but the other fifty per cent were male—and that partition persisted beyond meek conformity, in that fays who mated with human males usually only produced two children, one male and one female, before dying or changing form. The fay philosophers were unsure as to how to explain that, but many of them suspected that the mating was itself a kind of death sentence. The sentence was not necessarily executed swiftly, but it was rare for fays who gave birth to demifay children to see them reach the age of their majority before undergoing death or metamorphosis, and the fays usually showed accelerated signs of aging themselves.

The female children of matings between fays and humans did not seem to be of any particular interest to the fay philosophers, who mostly considered them to be merely spoiled or diminished fays, but the male children attracted more interest and curiosity, simply because they were something new and anomalous, They were of particular interest to the fay strategists intent on finding a means for the fay species to survive, because they seemed to have much more potential, in a human world that was, by an large, a man's world, either for the subversion and perversion of human society or for the possible survival of fay blood even beyond the final extinction of Broceliande's dream, as cuckoos in the human nest, capturing something of the substance of dull matter to alloy with the mercurial substance of fay flesh.

The questions and controversies remained, however, even as the numbers of the fays dwindled inexorably. Given that some fays, in some circumstances, could contrive to produce male demifay children, albeit in strictly limited numbers, how could they make strategic use of them and their demifay sisters, if at all?

Even if the surviving fays could come up with a plan, with or without a consensus between them, would they be able to carry it out in time?

And, perhaps most important of all, what might the last fragment of the dying dream contrive, independently of their conscious designs, if the dream were capable of contriving any kind of intention, direction or pattern at all?

It was a mystery.

From the viewpoint of the surviving fays in the rapidly-progressing human Age of Iron, in fact, it was *the* mystery. And whether it had a key or not, it was the mystery with which they had to live, of which they had to be a part.

V

The Story of the Storm

The story of the forest was an extremely complicated one, far beyond the comprehension of a young child like Chanterelle. Why did her mother tell it to her? Why did she tell it to her in secret, and in a language that was not the one she had been taught to speak?

Evidently, her mother thought it important to do it, and to do it in that way. Evidently, she wanted to plant the seeds of a future understanding in Chanterelle's mind long before they would be capable of germinating there. Presumably, she thought that she had to do it while the child was still a child because she did not expect to be able to do it later, because she expected something drastic to happen to her—or at least that something drastic might well happen to her—before Chanterelle reached an age at which she could have explained the story of the forest to her in a way that would make sense to a child or a young woman.

Whatever the reason, Chanterelle's mother obviously thought the story of the forest to be of such paramount importance that it needed to be told and retold incessantly, even if it would not be understood for a long time.

The other two stories that she thought vitally important were not nearly as complex and challenging, but it was still not easy to comprehend in their hidden significance, and they too would need to lie dormant for some time before Chanterelle could begin to get to grips with them.

The second one was the story of the storm, and this is the gist of it.

There was once a man who had to make a journey into the high forest in order to deliver an expensive musical instrument that he had been commissioned to make by a customer, which the customer called a "kithara": a stringed instrument reminiscent of a lyre, constructed to a design supplied by the customer and paid for in advance in gold: something highly unusual in the context of the trading practices of the day, which demonstrated a considerable level of confidence on the customer's part, especially as he—or she—had made the arrangement through intermediaries, and had never actually met the instrument-maker to whom the commission had been entrusted.

Because of that extraordinary trust confided to him, the instrument-maker—a young man who had not yet completed his apprenticeship—was absolutely determined that he must make the delivery personally and ensure the satisfaction of his mysterious customer, who had sent him very careful directions as to how to reach a delivery address in a hamlet high on a mountain, in a dense part of the forest where there was only one winding path connecting the hamlet to a broader path that was itself only a branch of a side-road that extended several leagues from the high road.

Unfortunately, as the young man was scaling the flank of the mountain, very carefully, on a horse that was not accustomed to such abrupt and rugged terrain, a terrible storm blew up, which produced a dramatic series of lightning flashes and a cacophony of thunderclaps that seemed to be almost directly overhead.

One lightning-bolt blasted a tall tree directly ahead of the horse, less than a hundred strides away. The animal reared up in panic, utterly terrified, threw its rider after the briefest of struggles, and bolted.

Perhaps absurdly, the young man's only thought, as he landed on the stony ground, was the necessity of protecting the musical instrument that he was delivering, which he had wrapped up in waterproof cloth much more securely than he was wrapped himself. Fortunately—at least from that point of view—he had strapped the instrument very carefully to his breast, and the horse threw him backwards, so that he was able to cushion the kithara from possible breakage, albeit while exposing his own spine to a dire threat. He had contrived to remove his feet from the stirrups when the horse reared up, though, and instead of falling directly on to his back—or, even worse, his head—he was able to simulate a kind of leap, which enabled him to land feet first before tumbling backwards. He jarred his ankles and the base of his backbone rather badly, and suffered multiple contusions, but he avoided smashing his skull or severing his spinal cord, and when he managed to get to his feet, he found that he could still walk, after a fashion.

It was pitch dark between lightning flashes, but the flashes were sufficiently frequent to give him a series of glimpses of the path, enabling him to continue to follow it, stumbling awkwardly, and completely drenched.

Shaken as he was, he soon lost track of time, and began putting one foot in front of the other automatically, dreading at every step that one or other of his aching ankles might give way and make it impossible for him to go any further. When he came to a bend in the path where the lightning showed him an overhanging rock, therefore, and a fissure that offered shelter from the wind and the rain, he edged himself into it, resolved to wait for the rain to stop, or at least to ease, trying in the meantime to convince himself that the fissure, being only just wide enough to accommodate a man and a kithara, could not be a bear's den or a wolves' lair.

The latter conjecture seemed to be correct, at least for as long as the storm lasted. When it began, it had brought abut a premature dusk, but by the time it blew over it really was the middle of the night. Fortunately, when the heavy clouds cleared, they revealed a moon. It was only three-quarters full, but it was high in the sky, and seconded by a seeming myriad of stars. By their light the young man was able to see the path and would have been able to keep following it, all the way to the hamlet that was his destination, if he had not been virtually lame.

When he emerged from the cleft however and limped back on the bend in the circuitous route, however, he caught a glimpse of a light some fifty or sixty paces to the side of the road, in the trees. He had no idea how much longer he might have to follow the path to get to the hamlet to which it led, but he was virtually certain that his ankles simply would not carry him much further, and that he might not even make fifty paces without abundant support from the trees.

He therefore left the path and headed for the light, praying that it was not deceptive, and really was that of a habitation.

As he drew closer to the source of the glimmer, he began to doubt its reality, because the pale white glow did not seem to be lamplight and the gap through which it was shining did not appear to be a window. The moonlight and starlight filtering through the canopy was not sufficient, however, for the young man to make out anything except the gleam itself, so he continued lurching toward it, and was within half a dozen paces when his legs finally gave out and he fell to his knees, clutching the kithara tightly in order to make sure that it came to no harm.

"Help!" he shouted. "For pity's sake!"

He became dizzy, and there were stars before his eyes, but he fought with all his might not to fall unconscious, and was vaguely aware of the sound of a door opening.

"Help!" he managed to call, again, and then tried to steady himself,

He felt a groping hand grip his—a very small hand—and a female voice said: "Can you walk, if I help you? It's only a few steps."

"I'll try," he promised.

And try he did. The presence of another seemingly-human being, albeit a frail girl who surely would not have been able to hold him up had he fallen, rendered him courage. He contrived to limp where the guiding hand took him, and reached the doorway from which she had emerged. Then he tumbled inside, before crawling to a kind of low couch, illuminated—barely and by no means brightly—by the strange white light he had perceived at a distance, gathered into a nebulous globe adherent to the wooden ceiling.

He managed to lie down on the couch, still cradling the carefully-wrapped kithara in his arms.

He could see the girl's face, albeit palely and a trifle uncertainly, and he wondered whether there might be something amiss with his eyes. It was, however, a very beautiful face. He had no doubt about that.

She fumbled with his boots, and finally contrived to pull them off, not without causing him a good deal of pain. Then she palpated his ankles carefully.

"Nasty bruises," was her eventual verdict, "but nothing broken. Let me take this, and take off your wet coat. I'll get you a blanket."

This was the kithara. She sensed his reluctance to let go of it, and said: "I'll put here, where you can see it. Don't worry. You have to get that wet coat off, though. Look, I'll put it over here."

He didn't bother to explain that he really wasn't worried about the coat, and was actually more concerned about the fact that the gloom was to intense for him to see where she put the kithara…or, indeed, anything else in what was presumably a cabin of some sort.

"You have no fire," he observed.

"No," she confirmed. "Jut a stove for cooking, which we don't usually keep alight at night." She gave him the promised blanket. It did not seem to be made of wool or animal-fur, although he could not tell what kind of thread it might have been woven from. He wrapped it around himself, though, and it seemed warm enough.

"What are you doing out here in the forest?" she asked him.

"Delivering a kithara to a mountain hamlet," he told her. "My horse was frightened by lightning, threw me and bolted."

"What's a kithara?"

"A musical instrument."

"This?" she asked, indicating the deep shadow in which she had presumably placed his precious package.

"Yes."

"It's better protected against the insults of the weather than you were," she observed.

"Yes," he agreed. "Is this where you live?" He peered into the strange pale gloom, but could not make out anything more than the vague outlines of a few items of furniture.

"Yes."

"Not alone?"

"No, of course not. My mother…how did you find the house?"

"I saw the light from the path. Oddly enough, it seemed brighter from there than it does now, at much closer range. Have you turned it down?"

"Not exactly," she replied. She leaned over to peer at him more closely, although he thought that she would need yes like a cat's in order to see him. He could barely make out the white oval of her face and her dark eyes and eyebrows. Her long hair seemed to be black, but had a slight silvery sheen in the equivocal light.

"You really saw it?" she queried.

"Yes, of course. How else could I have known that there was a habitation here?"

"I don't know," she admitted. "I thought…well, I don't know what I thought. A kithara, you say?"

"Yes."

"A musical instrument?"

"A kind of lyre, with seven strings, and a kind of frame I haven't seen before, perhaps designed by the customer who asked me to make it. I have a certain reputation, even though I'm still technically an apprentice, although I don't suppose it extends…but then, who would have thought that it would have reached as far as a mountain hamlet as remote as the one near here? My name is Alastor Ernand."

"Ernand!" It seemed to him that the pale silhouette started, and that the sweetly musical voice became discordant. "Ernand the Iron-master?"

The young man was not astonished that his father's reputation had extended so far, especially as his father had told him that he had heard of the hamlet to which he was traveling. "I'm his son," he said, without enthusiasm.

"Ah!"

"You've heard of my father, then, but not of me?"

"Everyone has heard of the iron-master," she replied. "You should not be here. I should not have answered your appeal. Except…."

"Except what?"

"How did you find this place? How did you see the light?"

"I don't know. It seemed quite bright, when I first glimpsed it. Now it seems almost extinct. But why shouldn't you have answered when I called for help? You can surely see that I'm not a brigand. I'm just a maker of musical instruments. I mean you no harm…and I can hardly walk."

"I'm not afraid of you," the spectral form assured him. "But…you might be in danger here."

"From your mother?"

"From Amanita."

"Who's Amanita?" asked the young man, although he might have guessed, given what his father had told him about the vicinity.

"It doesn't matter. I shouldn't even have mentioned her name. If she comes…Mother's gone to meet her. They might not come…but if she does…oh, what a fool I am! Tonight, of all nights. This is bad. I think they'll come…except that I wasn't thinking at all…but I could hardly leave you out there, could I, hardly able to walk, and drenched…and you have some kind of lyre. It must make sense somehow, but I can't see how. Perhaps Mother can work it out…she's a dream-reader. I'm just… well, I don't know what I am…."

"Calm down, please," the young man said. "I can't make head nor tail of what you're saying, but I don't want to get you into any kind of trouble. I can make it back to the path, I think. Do you know how far it is to the hamlet?"

"Too far," the girl muttered. "Much too far. No, I did the right thing…the only thing. If Amanita's angry, too bad…and she might not even come. But if she does, Mother will handle her. They're sisters, after all, not deadly enemies. Mother won't blame me…you were only half a dozen steps away, and you'd seen the light. You saw the light! That's strange."

"I don't see why," said the young man.

"I know…but you're the iron-master's son. That's bad. This shouldn't have happened. It shouldn't have been possible. I don't understand it at all…ah!"

For a moment, the young man thought that the girl had had a sudden inspiration that would help her to explain all the odd things she was saying—but then he realized that she had heard the sound of voices, approaching. They were female voices, slightly raised as if in anger, but they were speaking a language that the young man did not recognize and could not understand.

"Quickly," said the girl. "You have to get into the cupboard, and you have to be as quiet as a mouse—quieter! If she finds you, you might be in danger. She won't be here long, but while she is, you have to hide."

All the time, she was tugging his arm, and, not wanting to disoblige her in the least, he allowed himself to be guided and shoved exactly where she wanted him to go—which was, indeed, into some kind of cupboard, where there was just room to sit down with his knees tucked underneath his chin.

Then she piled the kithara on top of him, and his coat in top of the kithara, neither of which additions made his position any more comfortable.

She had barely managed to close the door on him before he heard the sound of another door opening, and the two voices that he had heard arguing outside were suddenly inside, still arguing in the unknown language.

From then on, for the next two hours, the young man did not understand a word that was spoken in the strange abode where he had somehow ended up, in a fashion that evidently seemed incomprehensible to the young woman who had let him in, even though he could not see anything particularly unusual about it himself, except perhaps that the light that had seemed bright when he glimpsed it from the path had grown dimmer as he approached it instead of brighter, as one would have expected.

All he could do now, he figured, was to comply as best he could with the girl's urgent request, and try to be as quiet as a mouse, or quieter.

Perhaps he did not quite manage, that, but the argument between the two women that had just come in was sufficiently heated for them not to notice trivial sounds, all the more so as the girl moved around herself, making noises that were unobtrusive in themselves, but adequate to cover any undue rustles and squeaks that he might make accidentally as he attempted to writhe in discomfort, in spite of the lack of room.

This is bizarre, he thought. *Can it possibly be a dream. Did I hit my head when I fell off the horse, and have I been unconscious ever since? No, obviously not. It hurts too much. No need to pinch myself to prove that I'm awake. This is real. But what is it? Why would this Amanita, of whom I've never heard, want to harm me? Why does it matter that I'm the iron-master's son, given that I've left home to be apprenticed to old Zebedee in the town?*

Such unanswerable questions at least occupied his mind while he tried to stay still, listening to the incomprehensible conversation as if in hope of catching the occasional word he knew, which might give him a clue to its subject matter.

All he could discern, however, was a set of four fluid syllables, repeated several times, which appeared to be a name:

"Lucinia."

He guessed that that was the girl's name. He also guessed, in consequence, that the two women were arguing about her. He guessed that the angrier of the two disputants must be Amanita, while the other must be Lucinia's mother—but that was as far as he got in trying to unravel the puzzle.

The girl was right, though. In the end, Amanita did not stay very long. He got the impression that she left in something of a huff. She had been gone for several minutes before the girl opened the door of the cupboard again, and the young man saw two dark figures silhouetted by the nebulous light, peering down at him.

Finally, the mother spoke in terms he could understand.

"Alastor Ernand," she said, "kithara-maker extraordinary. Now that *is* extraordinary."

He found that he could not unbend his cramped legs, let alone stand up.

"In fact," he said, "it's the first kithara I've ever been asked to make, and I had no idea what one was until I received the design. Usually, I make flutes and lutes."

"And mischief, it seems. If Amanita had found you…why on earth were you brought here?"

"I wasn't brought," he said, easing himself out while still in a folded position, and trying to stretch his legs. "I just stumbled. I'm truly sorry if I've caused you any inconvenience, and I'd be only too happy to leave, if I could only stand up and walk. Alas…"

"Stay," said Lucinia's mother, firmly. "Whether you were brought here for a reason or not, you're here. My daughter took you in, you have the right of hospitality. Can you get to that couch, if I offer you my arm?"

"I think so," the young man said. And he did—just in time to lose consciousness, finally, when he fell down upon it, and jarred his pain-racked limbs and back yet again.

VI

The Story of the Secret Place

Chanterelle realized the first time that her mother told her the story of the storm that it was an episode from her mother's own life, and that it concerned her mother's first meeting with her father. For that reason, if for no other, it seemed important, all the more so because her mother seemed reluctant to talk about such matters when the whole family was gathered—or, indeed, about anything touching vaguely on her origins.

On the other hand, Chanterelle could not see what there was about the story of the storm that made it so important from her mother's point of view that it had to be told in secret, or what connection it had to the story of the forest. She did, however, notice that the story, as told, had a conspicuous gap in it. The young man with the kithara had not understood a word of the conversation between Amanita and her sister, but her mother must have understood the words, at least, even if its meaning and significance had remained problematic. There was, in consequence, no reason why her mother could not fill in that gap in the narrative and explain to her young listener what the young man had overheard without being able to comprehend.

That was, however, the way the story went in her mother's secret telling. The gap was deliberate. Perhaps it would be filled in at another time, or perhaps there was some reason why her mother did not want Chanterelle to know, as yet, exactly why the two women had been at odds. Perhaps, Chanterelle thought, the argument had concerned her mother, and there was some personal secret that her mother wanted to keep, even from her beloved daughter, even while she was trying hard to provide their beloved daughter with the foundation-stones of a future enlightenment.

The third secret story that had particular importance to the teller and, implicitly for the listener, was a continuation of the second—or, more accurately, a sequel, since there was another gap between the events of the two stories in which certain significant things much have happened that were not spelled out. That third story was the story of the secret place, and it was interesting to Chanterelle not merely in itself but also because it connected with something her father had said about a recurrent dream he had—which, according to the story, had not begun as a dream at all… unless the story itself were a disguised account of a dream.

Again, this is the gist of the mother's telling of the story, or Chanterelle's memory of it, when she eventually began to glimpse its crucial relevance to her own life and possible future:

On the fourth day after his arrival in Melusine's abode, the young man with the kithara found that he was able to walk again with reasonable comfort and more than adequate strength to follow the road to the hamlet. When he expressed his intention of doing that, however. Melusine would not hear of it.

"No," she said, firmly, as she made him sit down at the table by the stove and ladled mushroom soup into a bowl for him. "You must stay here for one more day and night, and you shall not walk to the hamlet. You must ride."

"But you have no stable and no horse," the young man said. He had been able to walk far enough to sit outside when the sun was shining and the weather was good, so he had been able to see that the remarkable dwelling had no dependencies, and that the only animal that his hostess appeared to possess was a nanny-goat from which she obtained milk.

"That's one of the reasons why you must stay here one more day," said Melusine. "I have to procure you a horse, and that's not the simplest thing to accomplish out here."

"I might be able to buy one in the hamlet," the young man said.

"You might," Melusine agreed, "but when its people realize that you're stranded such a long way from home they will certainly not sell one to you cheaply. I, on the other hand, will give you a better one, saddled and harnessed, for nothing. Then you can ride to the hamlet, deliver the instrument, and ride all the way home afterwards in relative comfort."

The young man hesitated between asking her why she would do that and asking the other question that was hovering on his lips. He decided that there would be time for both—and, for that matter, several others that he had queued up while he was in the process of waking up on his improvised bed of moss and leaves, in the hope of obtaining answers to at least some of them before he took his leave of his taciturn hostess.

"What's the other reason that I have to stay for one more day?" he asked.

"Because, now that you can walk without the risk of any relapse, I want Lucinia to show you the secret place."

"What secret place?"

"It wouldn't be secret if I told you. You need to see it—and then you have to keep the secret."

"Wouldn't the secret be safer if you didn't show it to me…and it didn't even tell me that it existed?"

"Yes, it would. But secrets are only secret because they have a purpose. The point is not to bury them forever but to preserve them until the moment comes for them to be revealed to the right person, in the right circumstances.

"And I'm the right person?" said the young man, skeptically.

Melusine laughed. "Certainly not," she said, "But if I'm reading the dream correctly, you must be a link in the chain. I'm hoping that I *am* reading the dream correctly, because I'm staking a great deal on you, Alastor Ernand. There are some who might say that I was mad for doing so."

"Amanita?"

"To name but one. With luck, you'll never see her again."

"I've never actually seen her at all, because you or Lucinia always shut me up in the cupboard. You have no idea what a torment it is, being folded up like that when your feet are in agony. But she's your sister, so I imagine that she must look like you."

"Broadly speaking—but I look considerably older, and not nearly as beautiful. She can still be mistaken for a young woman, Lucinia's sister rather than mine."

"Mistaken?"

"She's older than she looks, while I've been…let's say, worn down by experience."

"She hasn't had any children, then?" the young man said, not meaning anything in particular by it, although he saw a slightly shift in Melusine's benign expression that was hard to pin down in terms of attributing it to any particular emotion.

"No," the woman replied. "She hasn't had any children."

The young man looked around, marveling once again at the fact that the little hut did not seem to contain anything that was not of vegetable origin: no metal, no glass, no ceramics. It was, technically speaking, a log cabin, but the "logs" of which it was made had not been sawn or planed, and had not been nailed of bolted. Absurd as it might seem, that seemed to have been fitted together like the sections of a jigsaw puzzle.

"Lucinia is out foraging, I assume," he remarked.

"Of course."

He looked down at his bowl, which was now almost empty, and the wooden spoon that he was using to ferry its contents to his mouth in measured doses. "Does she ever bring back anything but mushrooms?"

he asked.

"Of course. There are half a dozen different herbs in that as well as the goats' milk and the mushrooms, all medicinal—and the mushrooms include the very best of the forest's chanterelles. There's no better nutrition. Haven't your contusions healed, and don't you feel stronger and healthier now than you've ever felt before?"

"Well, yes," he admitted. "But I've hardly been able to credit that to a diet of mushrooms spiced with herbs. I suspect that it's a kind of magic, and that you're a witch—a white witch, obviously."

Again, Melusine's expression changed, into a wry smile. "It's an accusation I've heard before," she told him. "It's a trifle painful, to tell you the truth. I won't go so far as to say that there's no truth in it, but I don't cast spells."

"But you do tell fortunes?"

"Do I? What makes you think so?"

"You call yourself a dream-reader. Isn't at the same thing?"

Melusine sighed. "Perhaps it is," she said. "Whatever it is, I wish that I were better at it, for Melusinia's sake."

"Melusinia?"

"That's her full name—but I shouldn't have given it to her. It's too similar to my own, so I've modified it to Lucinia. One has to be careful with names, because they carry implications, which seem innocuous but sometimes aren't. You must always call her Lucinia."

"Always?" queried the young man, slightly surprised "Am I going to see her again, then?" He was being slightly disingenuous, He had every intention of seeing Lucinia again, but he was unsure, as yet, how Melusine might feel about that.

He found out very rapidly, when she replied, serenely: "When you've taken her to the town to marry her."

It occurred to the young man then that there as no longer any reason to ask why Melusine was not merely willing but anxious to supply him with a horse, on which he could ride comfortably. She intended him to carry a passenger. That surpassed the young man's vaguest intentions and hopes, but he was extremely glad to hear it.

"You must be a witch," he said. "I haven't even dared mention to her yet that I'm in love with her, and I have no idea what her response will be if I pluck up the courage to tell her."

"She might not know herself yet," said Melusine, serenely, "but she will when you ask, and I know already—because I'm her mother, not because I'm a witch."

"But you knew about me too!" the young man protested.

"That's obvious," she countered. "One would have to be blind not to see it, and deaf not to hear it in the way you speak to her. The secret place is ideal for confessions of that sort, by the way."

"Is that why you want her to take me to see it."

"No, but you might as well make use of the circumstance. Take your kithara."

The young man frowned. "It isn't my kithara," he said. "It belongs to the person who commissioned it, and paid for it in advance."

"But you have played it, haven't you?"

"I had to, in order to make sure of the honesty of the strings, and the working of the tuning pegs—not to mention the competence of the frame, although that's mostly in the design. And it would be an exaggeration to say that I played it. I've never played a seven-stringed instrument before, and I'm not much of a player anyway. I had to give it to my sister in order to get a perfect performance out of it and test the limit of its art. She's an infinitely better player than I am, and all instruments seem to come alike to her, including the most exotic."

"I think you'll find the secret place conducive to your own artistry," Melusine said, "And there's certainly no harm in trying the instrument one more time, to make sure that it didn't suffer any damage during the storm. But tell me more about your sister. She lives with you, then not the iron-master?"

"Yes. She didn't get on with him any better than I did. She loves music, and he has no time for it. She could hardly wait to come to live with me. We were very close as children, and are again now. Her name's Catrianne."

"Will she mind, do you think, when you take Lucinia home with you?"

"You seem to be taking a lot for granted there—but no, if I do take Lucinia home with me, I don't think Cat will mind at all. In fact, when she hears Lucinia sing…I think she'll want her for a sister almost as much as I'd like her for a wife, if she's willing."

"That's good," said Melusine. "It will be good for Lucinia to have a sister…very good, in fact…at least until your sister marries and has a family of her own."

"That could happen," the young man admitted. "Normally in fact, it would be expected….but I must admit that Cat doesn't seem to be at all interested in finding a husband. She's attracted admirers, but she puts them off. She always says that she isn't ready for marriage yet, but I can't help suspecting that she never will be. I think she has my father's example too much in mind, and can't convince herself that not all men are like that."

"I see. I hope you won't mind my saying so, but I like that too. I'd like Lucinia to have a sister who doesn't leave her in order to get married, someone to be her strong right arm. Lucinia isn't quite as strong as I could wish, you know…or as you will wish, in times to come."

"But your sister didn't leave you in order to marry, did she?" the young man probed, somewhat impertinently.

"No," said Melusine, with a slight sigh. "But Amanita's did, alas."

"Since you asked me about my sister," the young man persisted, "perhaps you won't mind if I ask you about yours. Why are you at odds? I confess that I find it frustrating to be stuck in that cramped cupboard listening to you argue, without being able to understand a word of it—except that you seem to be arguing about Lucinia."

Melusine laughed briefly, and humorlessly. "If only Lucinia were the only bone of contention! We disagree about almost everything, nowadays. She's my sister, and I love her, and in her way, I believe, she loves me, and Lucinia too—but I have to admit that beyond those two exceptions and a few others, she's a person deeply penetrated by hatred, capable of great malevolence. It's understandable that the local people call her a witch, even though she never does any lasting harm to the children she trains to sing. I know you think it absurd that I insist on hiding you from her, but I'm extremely glad that Lucinia made you hide on the night of the storm. If Amanita had found you here when we came in.…"

"But she can't possibly mean me any harm. She doesn't know me."

"I fear that she can. And I fear, too, that she'll be infinitely more capable of it once you've taken Lucinia away. In fact, I'll freely confess to you that one of the reasons that I'm so very enthusiastic to see you take her away is to remove her from Amanita's sphere of influence."

"One of the reasons?" the young man queried.

"Don't fish for compliments, Alastor—it's unbecoming. But yes, one of the reasons, not the only one.…but here comes Lucinia, with her basket. Be discreet now…but don't lack courage. It's necessary that you make a good start to your life together."

Lucinia brought in her basket, filled with an assortment of roots, leaves and fungal growths, which she handed to her mother. Melusine picked up the kithara from where it lay, still wrapped up, beside the makeshift bed that had been improvised for the unexpected visitor, and handed it to him.

"Go," she said. All that she added to that monosyllable, addressing her daughter, was: "Be careful."

Lucinia nodded, as if she understood exactly why she ought to be wary, although the young man was not at all sure.

The two of them set off into the forest, with Lucinia leading the way. They would not have been able to walk hand in hand even if the young man had not been carrying the instrument, because the undergrowth was too dense. The girl had no difficulty is finding a path through it, though, and seemed almost to be gliding, in sharp contrast to her companion, who tried had to follow exactly the same path but was continually caught in brambles or stumbling over roots. Mercifully, he contrived to keep the instrument safe from bruising impacts.

"I'm sorry," he said, at one point when he tripped badly, and she had to turn and extend a hand to him—or, to be strictly accurate, to the parcel containing the kithara, in order to help him steady himself. "You must think me very clumsy."

"Not at all," she said. "In fact, I find you rather puzzling. It's strange that you're able to get through this part of the forest at all, even with me to guide you. Are you sure that you're the iron-master's son?"

She did not mean anything by it, and blushed as soon as she realized that what she had said might be construed as casting aspersions on his mother. In the young man's opinion, however, the color seemed to suit her pale face very well, as a momentary change, and the way that she lowered her gaze in embarrassment seemed to add to the innate charm of her delicate beauty. The young man had never seen anyone like her, in the forest surrounding the foundry, in the town where he lived or in any of the other places he had visited.

He laughed lightly, in the hope of taking the edge of her embarrassment. "It's by no means the first time I've heard wonder expressed at the fact," he commented, "and I dare say that my father asked himself the same question more than once. But my sister is very similar to me in every respect that makes me different from my father, and I think he was forced by the coincidence to accept that the iron in his own blood had somehow failed to take priority over the blood transmitted to his wife by her father, who was a woodsman through and through."

"Woodsman?" the girl queried, as she continued leading him through the densent part of the forest, and he continue to follow her in spite of its apparent impenetrability."

"Yes, he was a woodcutter and charcoal burner, reckoned an expert feller and a clever distiller."

"Oh, she said. "That isn't what I meant." She sounded disappointed.

"In fact, her parentage was frequently doubted too," the young man added, "for the old crones of the neighborhood used to whisper that she was really a changeling: a fay child that had been switched in the cradle for the woodcutter's own daughter."

Lucinia stopped dead, and the young man had to take a step back in order not to run into her.

She turned round. "A changeling, you say?"

"It's a local superstition," he explained. "For some reason that I could never fathom, the fact that she died soon after giving birth to Catrianne encouraged the conviction. But you live among forest folk yourself—you must now how superstitious they are, especially with regard to the supposed activities of the fae-folk."

She stared at him, as if she were re-evaluating the idea that she had formed of him, and he was suddenly frightened, lest she think less of him for some reason, and less inclined to welcome the impending confession of his adoration.

"Have you told my mother that?" the girl asked.

"Yes, in fact, not long ago. She confessed that she had been the victim of slanderous rumors herself, but not of the same sort."

"No," said the girl, thoughtfully. "Not of the same sort." And she continued on her way, making no further comment until they reached the secret place.

The secret place was a clearing of sorts, or perhaps an arena, in which a circular space that appeared at first glance to be carpeted with moss and flowering plants was surrounded by a ring of trees so closely packed that they seemed to the young man to be reminiscent of the stout columns of a colonnade, their crowns overlapping to such an extent that they seemed to form an unbroken torus of verdure. That torus was some way above his head, though, because the thick boles of the trees extended to twice the height of a man, uninterrupted by branches.

When the young man stepped into the ring he hesitated, because the ground beneath his feet, although it looked innocuous enough, seemed to stir slightly as he stepped on it. After testing it, though, he decided that it was firm enough to support him, and he turned his attention to the surrounding trees.

The boles were not bare, because their thick, dark bark was engraved with characters of several different kinds, in astounding confusion—far too many to count, although they had to run into the millions. The young man did not recognize any of the symbols, and could not even tell whether they were letter or numbers, although there were some complex ones that might have been pictograms of a sort.

"My God," he said. "This must have taken an entire legion of sculptors decades—perhaps centuries—to contrive. He stepped closer to one of the trees and inspected the symbols at close range.

"This wasn't done with a metal chisel," he declared, confident in his expertise.

"No," agreed the girl. "My people don't use metal."

"Bone, then? All this was done with pointed bone-fragments?"

"Yes."

"Centuries, then. I'm a master woodworker, but I couldn't contrive work of this intricacy and delicacy with anything less than the finest bronze knives. This is positively amazing. But what is it?"

"A project undertaken by some of my people, begun a long time ago, when they first realized that the forest was sick, but had not anticipated how terrible the sickness would be. They thought…well, it doesn't matter what they thought, as they were wrong. They wanted to make a record—a history, so that those who came after them would have a legacy of their achievements. They were optimistic, I fear…but perhaps with more justification than some of us have recently thought."

"Can you read it all?"

"By no means all of it, I fear, and some of it only imperfectly. But with study, I think, and concentration, I could learn more. The characters have a certain facility in making themselves understood, to those who want to understand."

"Really? That sounds like magic to me."

"Perhaps, but I think that I can prove it to you…provided that you do want to understand."

"The words, you mean?"

"No, the music. Here, you see, there are indications of musical notes. There's only a limited number of ways that notes and the relationships between them can be expressed."

The young man realized why Melusine had insisted that he bring the kithara—but he felt completely out of his depth, convinced that he could not do what was being asked of him.

"But I can't read music, even in the way composers in my own town write it down," he protested. "I can only play by ear."

"I'm not sure that it would be an advantage if you could," Lucinia said. "What is necessary, I think, is that you want to understand. I think you do."

He did not voice the question, but he looked at her in a fashion imploring a further explanation.

"I think," she said, carefully, "that you want to understand *me*."

He nodded his head slowly. "Yes," he said, "that, I certainly do want. Is it really so obvious?"

"I fear so," she said, with a tiny smile. "Mother saw it on the very first night, when you'd hardly glimpsed me by nightlight."

"And if I can do this—if I can somehow contrive to read, and play, the music supposedly inscribed on that tree, then I'll understand you."

"Oh, that might take a very long time," she said, "but if you could read the music, it might be a good beginning."

"And if I can't."

"It's not a test, Alastor. If you have a question to ask me, it won't make any difference to the answer."

"Which is?" he asked, unable to contrive more than two syllables, for the moment.

This time the laugh was not as tiny. "You haven't asked me the question yet," she pointed out.

"True," he admitted. "Well, then...although I've only been here a matter of days...I've become exceedingly fond of you, beautiful Lucinia...and...I'd like to be allowed to pay court to you...."

"You mean that you'd like me to go away with you?"

"Not necessarily," he hastened to add. "If you need time...but I'd like to continue to see you...often...and ultimately...to ask your mother for your hand."

"Oh, don't worry about that," said the girl. "She'll be out searching for a horse by now. But when you say *not necessarily* I fear that you're mistaken. It *is* necessary, if you want me, for you to take me away, to-morrow at the latest. Is that too soon for you? Do you need more time?"

The young man pulled himself together. "No," he said, not knowing whether he was being courageous or not. "Absolutely not. If your mother can procure a horse, I'll gladly take you with me this very afternoon. But your mother...."

"Mother has to stay here," she said flatly. "And I have to leave. We've said our farewells and shed our tears. There's nothing left to do but let the dream take its course."

The young man gulped. "Yes," he said, "it does seem like a dream, doesn't it. *All* of this."

His hand gesture took in not merely the secret place, the elaborate-ly carved tree-boles, and Lucinia herself, but also, by implication, the strange cabin, and the forest itself, not excluding him and the musical instrument that he had been asked to make.

"It will," said the girl, with what might have been a slight sigh.

Almost without thinking about it, the young man had started un-wrapping the kithara. For the first time since he had left his workshop, he exposed it to the light, and showed it to the girl. She looked at it with great interest, and stroked the strings lightly with her delicate fingers.

"Have you seen anything like it before?" he asked.

"No," she replied.

"It's Greek, I believe. According to my Master, Zebedee, lyres start-ed out with only two strings, but the players kept adding more and more, until they ended up with the seven of the kithara—although he thinks there must have been experiments carried out with even more, ultimately resulting in the development of harps. Modern stringed instruments seem to find four or six adequate. It's very strange that someone living in what must be the remotest hamlet in the realm should have wanted me to make one. Zebedee says that it must be a philosopher and antiquarian retired to the heights in search of solitude, like the eremites of the old Thébaïd."

"That's possible," said the girl, withdrawing her hand from the instrument.

"Do you have another possibility in mind?"

"Perhaps."

"Amanita?"

Lucinia raised her eyebrows. "What makes you say that?" she parried, in a fashion that was not quite worth as much as an assent.

"Just a guess," he said, honestly.

"She hasn't said anything to us," the girl mused. "Mother's probably burning to ask, but doesn't dare. If, by chance, it was her, or one of her associates, for some reason that I can't fathom and Mother would be too cautious to voice, if all she had was a suspicion, then it wouldn't have been a good idea to drop the slightest hint that we knew about it."

"Isn't it a risk for me to try to play it, then? Someone might hear me."

Lucinia shook her head. "No one will hear us," she said. "That I can guarantee. This is the secret place; it can keep its secrets."

"And yet I'm here," said he young man.

"Yes, you are," his bride-to-be agreed. "And for that, there surely must be a reason. The dream is full of inconsequentialities, and it's dying, but even so…we must at least believe that there is some kind of meaning in its apparent madness, else all is lost. Fix your eyes on the tree, Alastor. Ask to understand, beg if you think it will help. And play."

She was asking too much. First, the young man had to tune the instrument, and play a few sample chords—with his fingers, for he had not detached the plectrum from its niche. He preferred to play lyres with his fingers, because it gave him a greater sense of intimacy with the instrument. Then, with the fingers of his right hand—the one with which he was going to pluck the strings—he reached up and ran the tips over the characters that, according to what Lucinia had told him, represented musical notes.

At first, all he could feel was the quality of the workmanship—but that was a key of sorts, because what guided his own workmanship was a kind of identification with the wood, and an attempt, however fanciful, to read the hidden intentions of its soul. He ran his fingers over the notches and groves until he found one that seemed, by its texture and position, to be the top E, the chanterelle, the one that was used as the tuning reference. Then he played that E on the kithara.

The process of interpretation did not go smoothly thereafter. He stumbled and he erred, producing little more than a cacophony for at least ten minutes—he lost track of time, so absorbed was he in his quest—but eventually, he found a sequence of chords that was almost mellifluous, and after that, his confidence was acquired.

At least, his confidence in the music was acquired, because as soon as he began to play, it seemed that he felt the ground beneath his feet stir again. He moved away slightly, toward the center of the arena, but the carpet of moss—which, he now felt sure, was not a carpet of moss at all, felt even less secure.

"Try to put it out of your mind," said Lucinia. "It won't let you sink. It will keep you safe—but as you play, and it absorbs the music, it will change. Please don't be afraid."

The young man did not want to show any fear before the young woman to whom he had just confessed his love, and who had agreed to go away with him, but he did want to show that he trusted her, so he tried to put all uncertainty about the floor of the secret place out of his mind, and concentrate on the music.

It worked. As the music developed in fits and starts, in fact, and absorbed all his attention, he lost any sense of where he was.

After what must have been nearly three-quarters of an hour, he finally turned to the girl, who was waiting, quite still, as if in a kind of trance, and said: "I think I can try to play the music, now. What I produce might be the product of my imagination rather than what's actually written on the tree, but I think I have something."

"Play," she said, again.

So he played, and she sang.

When he began to play he was still hesitant, and uncertain, half-convinced that he was only making it up, putting on an act because, even though she had said that it was not a test, he was desperate not to disappoint her. As soon as she began to sing, though, he felt sure that he was right, that he really was doing the impossible. He was not simply responding to her voice, because he was accompanying her simultaneously, but the confirmation provided by her notes—knowing, as he did, that she really could read the notes inscribed on the tree—reassured him that his inspiration was genuine.

He could no longer feel the ground beneath his feet; he felt that he had lost all contact with the earth: that he was floating, or soaring like a bird, like a great white swan, and that Lucinia was flying with him, beyond the limits of the world he knew.

He had no idea how long he played. He was lost, entranced, seemingly outside of time and space...except that time continued to fly by, and if the height of the sun could be believed—and how could it be disbelieved?—by the time that the finished playing, it was late afternoon.

He was dazed, almost stunned.

"There," said Lucinia. "I really didn't believe that you could do it, although mother told me to wait and see, and to hope—but I think you not only read the dream, but enabled it to find its own path, its own direction."

"I have no idea what that means," the young man said, "or what it is that you think I might have done."

She smiled. "You've played a song," she told him, "and I've sung it. That's our part. As for the rest…only time will tell."

"And what difference will it make, in the great scheme of things, when time eventually tells?"

"I have no idea," she said. "And if Mother has some inkling, she won't confide it to us, because she won't be sure. But wasn't it beautiful?"

Oddly enough, he had been concentrating so hard, that it had not even occurred to him to appraise it, even though he could feel its emotional resonances still surging through his blood and his fibers.

"Yes it was," he confirmed, having no doubt that it was an accurate assessment.

Then they kissed, for the first time. They had come back to earth, but they hastened to step out of the strange arena before the ground began to seem unsteady beneath their feet again.

There was no longer any chance that he could deliver the kithara before nightfall, let alone that he could make a start on the journey home. As Melusine had predicted, he had to postpone his departure until the following day, but that was no hardship, in the circumstances.

Soon after daybreak, the young man rode the horse that Melusine had procured for him to the hamlet, and delivered the kithara to the home of the agent who had brought him the commission. The agent who received it—obviously an intermediary—did not complain about the lateness of the delivery, although he seemed very relieved to see the instrument arrive. "Have you tested it?" he asked Alastor.

"Thoroughly," the instrument-maker replied. "Although I've never made one like it before, I think I can say without boasting that it's truly exceptional. It can make fine music."

"Good," said the agent, without attempting to try the kithara himself, and bowed to bid him farewell.

When the young man reached the point in the winding path where he had taken shelter from the storm, he found Lucinia waiting in the fissure that was not a bear's den. She leapt up behind him, very nimbly, even though she had a bag slung over her shoulder, and they rode away down the mountain at a steady trot, never to return.

VII

The Plague

All was well in Alastor's family until the plague came.

"It's not as terrible a plague as some," Alastor said to Catrianne, when the first people in the town fell victim to it. "It's not as rapacious as the one in the story of the great black spider—the one that terrified and blighted a highland village, infecting the inhabitants with fevers that sucked the blood and the life from every last one. This is a disease that the strong and the lucky may resist, if fortune favors them. Even so, we must try to avoid contact with the places that the disease has appeared, for fear of contagion."

That was far easier said than done, in a town where people were very busy, and came in contact with one another a great deal in the course of their daily activities. The Maire of the town ordered houses in which the disease had struck to be fumigated with odorous smoke, in the hope of choking the contagion, and the churches had never been so full or echoed so loudly with hymns or prayers, but neither smoke nor piety seemed able to check the spread of the disease.

Handsel was the first member of the family to come down with a fever, but the disease had been rife for some time by then, and it was already evident that most of the people who died of it were either very old, very young or possessed of some preliminary weakness that made it harder for them to survive the crisis of the fever. Handsel was twelve years old by then, and very sturdy; his parents and his aunt were very hopeful that they could nurse him through the fever successfully.

"We must do what we can to help fortune," Catrianne said. "We must pray, and we must give him watered wine or small beer to replace the sweat pouring out of him. He is strong; dozens weaker have already survived the malady."

The instrument-maker and his wife prayed, and they nursed poor Handsel as best they could—but within two days, Chanterelle had caught the fever too. Alastor and Catrianne redoubled their efforts, praying and nursing, fighting with every fiber of flesh and conviction of spirit for the lives both of their children.

Fortune favored them, at least to the extent of granting their most fervent wishes. Handsel recovered from the fever, and so did Chanterelle—but before Handsel had recovered, old Zebedee fell ill, and he was not so fortunate. The fever carried him off within twenty-four hours. Catrianne and Alastor both tried to nurse him by turns, while Lucinia remained in the house with her children, but then Lucinia came down with the fever too, rapidly followed by Catrianne and by Alastor.

They did their best to nurse one another, but soon, the roles were effectively reversed; it was the turn of Handsel and Chanterelle to look after their parents and their aunt. They tended the fire, boiled water, picked vegetables, cooked meat, and made sure that all three of the adults drank plenty of watered wine and small beer. They ran hither and yon in search of bread, blankets and candles, and they prayed with all the fervor of their young hearts and high voices.

Like consummate diplomats, they suppressed the terrible news that while Zebedee's house was being fumigated following the removal of his body on the plague-cart, wood-dust and chippings in Alastor's workshop had caught fire, and the whole house had gone up like a torch, which the firemen were unable to put out. Indeed, they had had enormous difficulty preventing it from spreading to its neighbors.

All of Alastor's tools, and all his works in progress, were destroyed.

He was never told that it had happened, but Handsel suspected that he had somehow known that something bad had occurred, and that the impact of the news, although presumably not fatal in itself, had combined with the height of the crisis of the illness. Although he was certainly not the weakest member of the family, and anyone looking at the five of them would immediately have indentified him as the strongest, Alastor died of the plague.

Perhaps Lucinia, in spite of her evident delicacy, might have pulled through if Alastor had recovered sufficiently to sit by her bedside and lend her his moral support, and the others tried to keep the news of his death from her, just as they had tried to keep the news of the destruction of his workshop from Alastor—but she knew. It was not simply that she had a suspicion; the moment that Alastor expired, she *knew*, and it appeared to the children and their aunt that the knowledge killed her, as surely as a dagger in the heart. She lingered for another twenty-four hours, although she seemed to age thirty years in the space of that single day, and died resembling a crone, but the children, who seemed to have grown to a premature adulthood themselves in a matter of a few days, could do nothing to save her.

They feared, inevitably, that they would lose Catrianne as well, who deduced her brother's death easily enough, and seemed to know as soon as she had made the deduction that Lucinia could not survive the blow. Instead of crushing her as well, however, it seemed to make her determination to live stronger. Apparently, there was honest iron in her soul, which must have come from her father. She told herself, and told Handsel and Chanterelle too, that she simply *could not* die, that she had to live, for their sake, because they must not be left alone in the world.

The children were apologetic about the death of their parents.

"I wasn't strong enough," Handsel lamented. "My hands weren't clever enough to do what needed to be done."

"My voice wasn't sweet enough," mourned Chanterelle. "My prayers weren't lovely enough for Heaven to hear them."

"You mustn't think that," Catrianne said to them, while she was still in bed, very weak but out of danger. "Neither of you is at fault in any way. You did everything humanly possible. You kept me alive, and you still are keeping me alive. I couldn't have survived without you."

They assured her that they understood that they had done nothing wrong, and had not failed their father or their mother in any way—and it seemed that Handsel, perhaps because he was the elder, really did understand that. From that day on, however, Chanterelle claimed that she could no longer sing.

Catrianne did everything she could to coax the little girl out of her silence, but nothing worked. She could not help thinking, no matter how had she tried, about the tale about the man who knew the secret of making nightingales sing by day, and what he did when the little girl in the story eventually refused to sing. She realized that Lucinia had been right to warn her that once she knew the end of the tale, she could never unlearn it again, and that it would haunt her forever. Even though she could not believe, even in the context of the tale, that the wicked old man would ever have done to the lovely child what he had earlier done to the nightingales—run hot needles into her eyes in order to blind her—and certainly had no intention of telling Chanterelle the story, ever since Chanterelle had stopped singing, she could free herself from the haunting of the image, and the superstitious suspicion that it somehow constituted a bad omen. She could not suppose for an instant that anyone would ever want to blind Chanterelle, but the tale seemed symbolic nevertheless of some mysterious threat hanging over her.

Catrianne wondered such a story had ever been imagined, given that it did not have the happy ending that stories ought to have, but realized belatedly that was precisely the reason: the maker of the tale had wanted to display the conviction that the happy endings attached to tales were essentially unrealistic, and that in the real world, plagues struck down the just as well as the unjust, and left the innocent to fend for themselves, without the wherewithal to do it, instead of the guilty, who were better equipped to survive at the expense of their fellows, simply because there were not innocent.

In fact, Catrianne said to herself, in order to fight the haunting, *I don't believe that little girl began to sing again for any other reason than because she wanted to recover the joy of it. I don't think it had anything to do with the wicked old man.* But she had a hard time maintaining that unbelief.

Chanterelle, however seemed to have despaired of recovering the joy of song. She would not rejoin the choir at the church, nor would she sing at home, either by day or by night, no matter how hard Catrianne and Handsel tried to seduce her voice with their tunes.

In fact, they did not try very hard, because as soon as Catrianne was fully recovered, she realized the dire circumstances the family was now in. They had exhausted their savings while caring for the various invalids, one after another or several at a time. With the workshop and its contents utterly destroyed, all that they had to sell was the contents of the house, and then the house itself.

Handsel, at twelve, had already cultivated a certain skill, by the standards of a raw apprentice, but he had no tools, and even if they had used up some of their resources to buy him tools and raw materials, there was no guarantee that the kind of work he was capable of doing could make sufficient income to sustain them—quite the contrary. Catrianne was an expert player, and still owned several musical instruments, but in the wake of the plague, the ravages of which had severely disrupted the economy of the town, there were few opportunities to earn money as a musician, even by playing on street corners and effectively becoming a beggar.

"I don't think we can stay here," she explained to the children. "We can live for a few weeks, perhaps months, but once we have nothing left to sell but the house itself, we'll be homeless. So far as I can see, we have only one viable option, one place to which we can turn to help."

"What's that?" asked Handsel.

"We have to go to my father's foundry, and appeal to him for help. I haven't seen him for nearly fifteen years, and he's never seen either of you, but I'm his daughter and you're his grandchildren. Even a man with a heart of iron couldn't turn us away. He'll be able to find you a new apprenticeship, Handsel, or even give you one, if you're willing and able to turn your hand to ironwork, and he'll supply you, Chanterelle, with a home and an education at least until you're old enough to marry. What he'll do with me, I don't know. I'm past thirty now, but perhaps not entirely unmarriageable, if desperation drives me to that, and again, he won't let me starve while investigations are made. He's old himself now, and it's entirely possible that he'll be grateful to have me as a housekeeper, to care for him in his dotage."

"Is that really all we can do?" Handsel asked.

"Alas, yes. My other grandfather is long dead."

"What about mother's family?"

"I never met her mother, and I don't believe that Alastor ever heard a word from her after he left her house with Lucinia. There was some mystery about it that neither of them ever wanted to explain, and I can't begin to understand, but what's certain is that neither of them, so far as I know, ever made the slightest attempt to contact her. I have no idea how to find her, if she's still alive, and only a vague idea of where I might start looking. All I know is that her name was Melusine, that she lived in the vicinity of a hamlet in the remotest part of the highlands, and that she had a sister named Amanita. I suppose I can locate the hamlet on a map, so that if my father were unkind enough to turn us away, we could keep on going along the road. I could certainly try to find my way to the right mountain, where we could ask for her or her sister, but that would be a desperate measure, and I really can't believe that my father would turn us away."

"Amanita was bad," Chanterelle put in.

"What do you mean, darling?"

"Amanita was bad—wicked. Melusine sent my mother away in secret because she didn't want Amanita to know where she'd gone, or who with."

"How do you know that, darling?"

"Mother told me a story."

"A story?"

"Yes. She told me stories sometimes. She told me the story of how she and father met, and the story of how they went to the secret place."

"The secret place?"

"Yes. The place that father thought was a dream, but wasn't."

Catrianne thought about that, not knowing what to make of it, and not knowing whether, in view of the fact that Chanterelle had qualified it as a story, it was fiction or fact. She decided, however, that it probably didn't matter, given that she had no intention of going to look for Melusine, let alone her evil sister.

She couldn't help being slightly piqued, however, by the revelation that Lucinia seemed to have told her young daughter more about her past life than she had ever told her, and she was more than a little curious.

"Did she tell you anything else about Melusine?" she asked.

"She was a dream-reader."

"A fortune-teller, you mean?"

"No. I'm not sure, but I don't think she read people's dreams—just the dreams of Broceliande."

"Who's Broceliande?"

"The forest—the great forest that dreamed the fae-folk."

Fiction, then, Catrianne thought. *Just stories—but perhaps with a grain of truth in them, or at least of meaning. After all it's not impossible that Lucinia's mother imagined that she could read and interpret the dreams of the forest. There are crazier people than that even in the town.*

"Did your mother ever say anything about this to you, Handsel?" she asked.

"No," said Handsel, who seemed more than a little piqued himself to have been left out of that part of his mother's confidences, "but Father told me—told us all, in fact—how he met Mother in the mountains when he was delivering an instrument he called a kithara, and how they fell in love as soon as they saw one another, and rode away together as soon as he'd delivered the instrument."

"I remember the kithara," Catrianne said. "He asked me to play it, to test it. A beautiful instrument. I've never seen its like again—a great pity."

"Father played it in the secret place," Chanterelle put in.

"The place that he thought was a dream, but wasn't?"

"Yes. Mother sang. It was important, but I don't understand why. Mother thought the kithara might have been ordered by Amanita, but she wasn't sure. They had to hide Father in a cupboard so that Amanita didn't see him. If she had, something bad would have happened"

"What?" asked Handsel.

"I don't know, but bad."

"I wish your mother had told me these stories," Catrianne said, pensively. "I would have liked to know her a little better than I was allowed to, considering that we were practically sisters. I didn't keep any secrets from her."

"She couldn't tell you or Handsel," said Chanterelle "You couldn't understand the secret language."

"What secret language?"

"The secret language the stories were in."

"And you could?"

"Yes. I don't know how. The same way Father understood the music written on the trees, I suppose, although it was much harder for him."

"I suppose so," said Catrianne, deciding that the conversation had become too gnomic to be worth continuing, although she made a mental note to return to the topic when she had the leisure to do so. "In any case," she went on, "the simple fact is that we have to go. There's no point in hanging on here until our resources are exhausted. "We need to set out for the foundry now, while the days are still long and the nights still relatively short, because the journey will soon get more difficult as summer ends and autumn begins. It's a long journey to make on foot, but no one will rent us a trap to make it, as we won't be coming back. Do you think you're capable of walking that far, if we take it in relatively easy stages? I know you're both weak after the fever—I'm weak myself—but the sooner we go, the better. Are you ready? You'll need to be brave, but if the last two months have proved anything, they've proved that. Are you with me?"

"Yes, Aunt Cat," said Handsel, stoutly.

"Yes," said Chanterelle, simply.

And thus the matter was decided.

VIII

The Foundry

The journey to the highlands was long and by no means easy, because all three of them were still physically weak from the effects of the plague, and spiritually desolate because of the loss of Alastor and Lucinia. The children had watched both their parents die, while making every effort they could to save them, while Catrianne had lost a brother to whom, in the fashion that she interpreted her own feelings, she had always been so close that she had never had the slightest interest in other men, and a sister-in-law who had been as much to her as any actual sister. The void left in their lives was terrible.

What made the matter worse, from Catrianne's viewpoint, was that she could not think of the destination toward which they were heading as any kind of substitute for what they had lost. She hoped that it would provide a safe haven for the children, and that Ernand would feed them and keep them secure while they grew through the six years or thereabouts that would bring them to the advent of maturity, and hence preserve the potential they had to seek and find lives of their own. As she had told them, that protection would preserve for Handsel the potential of finding and completing a satisfactory apprenticeship, and for Chanterelle the potential of making a good marriage, and hence the possibility for both of them of a satisfying role in society. For her, however, it did not seem to offer anything at all.

The role that Catrianne had wanted, and had made for herself, albeit without ever formulating the ambition unconsciously, during the decade and more of her own adulthood, had been the role she played as an adjunct to her brother's family. That had allowed her to play her instruments, without requiring to earn money for so doing, and to assist in domestic labor and the education of the children without having to accept the heavier duties of a wife and mother. Doubtless she would be able to continue her assistance with the care and education of Handsel and Chanterelle, for a while, but beyond that, all that life in the foundry seemed to offer was a bleak and somber existence, which she had only been able to tolerate in childhood because Alastor's presence had provided it with light, and love, and purpose. What substitute could she possibly find for that?

Her dejection was not absolute, however.

The road that the three of them had to follow was just a road, something hard that hurt their feet, unused to walking long distances, full of dust and people, as bleak in itself as the condition of her soul; but the route, which initially ran between buildings and then between cultivated fields, soon plunged into the forest, which soon became dense to either side. There were all kinds of accessories to the road, at intervals: inns and relay stations, little clusters of dwellings and mercantile operations gathered around a blacksmith's forge or a spring, but they were mere excrescences on the edges of the wound that cut through the forest's heart. Usually, the forest came to the very edge of the highway, and was never more than a few paces away.

Somehow, while living in the town, with Alastor, Catrianne had contrived, if not to forget the forest, at least to put it behind her, to separate herself from it. She had not realized how much she had missed it, and was surprised, therefore, to find a feeling of familiarity and belonging as she moved into it and through it. Strangely enough, the children, who had never been in the forest, seemed to feel something similar; it could not, for them, be an authentic familiarity, because they only knew the forest in tales they had been told, but that oblique acquaintance nevertheless seemed to allow them to feel a sense of belonging.

All three of them felt that they were more comfortable on stretches of the road where there was little traffic and no gangs of pavers working on its incessant maintenance. Although Catrianne insisted that they spend the nights of their three-stage journey in the common-rooms of inns, huddled together on a rolled-out mattress, in the company of other travelers, instead of yielding to Handsel's suggestion that they spend them under bushes or on beds of moss, she could not suppress a strange and surely irrational conviction that they would not only be more comfortable with nothing between them and the stars but the forest canopy, but also safer.

The journey was made more difficult that it would have been for a single adult traveler because all three of them had to adapt their stride and their pace to Chanterelle's. It did not help that the road was by no means level. It went up hills and down, but the sum of its various climbs and dips was always upwards as they moved further into the highlands. Then again, the plague, which had arrived in the town via the road, continued its own travels by the same means. It seemed to have left the highest ground almost untouched untouched, for fevers did not seem to feel at home on places that were too high on a hill, but it had insinuated itself into all the valleys, sometimes descending on the villages with unusual ferocity.

When Catrianne began to sense that pattern, she began to feel another anxiety gnawing away at her. The plague had evidently traveled faster than the meager pace that they were able to maintain, and it had had well over a month's start on them. It was afflicting populated places in regions hollowed out by mountain streams and rivulets with a particular hostility.

What ravages, then, would it have perpetrated on a huge clearing in which the foundry and the cluster of habitations and industrial operations surrounding it were situated?

It did not take long for that anxiety to be transformed into a real fear, and an ominous foreboding. It did no good for Catrianne to tell herself that her father was a strong and sturdy man, only on the threshold of old age: a man of iron. After all, his son had been a strong man too, still in his prime, and the fever had not spared him.

And her fear, alas, proved all too justified.

It was dusk when the exhausted Catrianne and her children, after a long stage that had brought them to the limit of their endurance, finally reached the clearing where the foundry stood, and presented themselves at its gates.

They found the gates closed, and the buildings dark and deserted. No work was being done there, and no one was in residence.

The gates were impenetrable, but the fence surrounding the property was mostly rotten, a boundary-marker rather than a barrier. Catrianne had no difficult getting into the property, or the house in which she had grown up. There was no one inside, but at least she found materials with which to build a fire in the kitchen range, a good supply of tallow candles, taps from which water still ran and comfortable beds on which to lie down. In her old room, which did not seem to have been touched, let alone inhabited, since she had gone to join Alastor some fifteen years before, she found long-forgotten possessions: clothing, trinkets and toys. Most of the clothes had been eaten away by moths, but she searched the other rooms with the aid of a lantern, and managed to assemble a collection of garments that had been carefully packed for preservation, of which she and the children could make good use.

There were not as many metal implements as she might have expected—clearly, much material of that sort had been removed by other hands—but she did not bother to collect those, even though common sense suggested to her that it might be wise to equip herself and the children with good knives. She was far more concerned to find good shoes, even though she did not expect to make any significant use of them for at least a few days. Their feet were blistered and sore, and would need several days to recover—as would their exhausted bodies.

Catrianne heated water so that they could all wash themselves thoroughly, and then put the children to bed. They were too tired to want to talk at length, but there were questions too urgent not to be asked.

"Are we going to stay here?" Handsel asked.

"If we can," Catrianne told him. "I'll need to make enquiries at the village church tomorrow, but the curé will be able to tell me where my father has gone, if he is still alive, and the terms of his testament, if he is not. It's possible that the foundry is mine now, and the house. If not... well, no one else is using it or the moment, and no one hereabouts is likely to dispute my right to be here."

"But what are we going to do?" the boy asked, plaintively.

"I don't know," she told him. "First, we have to discover what the possibilities are."

The children were too weary not to be able to sleep. Catrianne even contrived to sleep herself, although she had nightmares.

She did not get up until the sun was clear of the horizon, but she went out as soon as she felt able to do so. Her first priority was to buy bread and milk, in order to feed the children, which she did easily enough.

Many of the neighbors were already up and about. As she came out of the baker's shop she greeted two old crones that she remembered, who hardly seemed to have changed in a decade and more. They did not recognize her immediately, but acknowledged her as soon as she introduced herself, and a small group quickly formed, composed of women similarly out buying bread for the households they kept. They immediately asked after Alastor, and reacted to her revelation in kind.

She did not have to go as far as the church, therefore, to begin hearing the catalogue of the village's woes. The women surrounding her were only too ready to detail their own losses of husbands, siblings and children. The catalogue of catastrophe was so prompt and so extensive that it took long minutes for Catrianne to find an opportunity to ask about her father, but when she did, and was told that he was not among the plague's victims, the flicker of hope that burst forth in her frightened mind in response to that information was soon quenched.

"Your father," one of the crones said, "had gone mad some time before the plague arrived. For years he had been sullen and morose—your brother must have told you that he found him thus whenever he came to see him—and he seemed gradually to lose interest in the foundry. The decline was slow, but it only went from bad to worse. Then, one day, he simply abandoned everything, and left."

"Where did he go?" asked Catrianne.

The crone hesitated, before saying: "No one knows."

"But you must have some idea," Catrianne objected.

"Oh, ideas," said the old woman. "No shortage of those. Whenever no one knows, everyone makes up stories, especially when there's bad blood."

"Bad blood?"

"I fear so, Mamzelle Catrianne. The men hereabouts all used to work in the quarry, the old mine and the foundry, but they were still forest folk at heart, and the forest has always been on our doorstep. Your father, although he was a man who loved iron, seemed to like that about us once. He married a woodcutter's daughter, after all—your mother, God rest her soul. Between the two of us, through, Alastor was a sore disappointment to him, and after he had gone…well, you probably remember yourself…."

"Remember what, exactly?" Catrianne asked, warily.

"Well, not that I ever believed it myself, you understand, but there were some who'd often said that your mother was a changeling, fae inside in spite of her human appearance, and that….forgive me, Mamzelle, you were half-fay yourself. You father had always ranted against such notions, calling them nonsense, but…."

"But what?"

"But it seems to me that he began to believe it—not because of you, Mamzelle, almost an angel, but because of Alastor and his liking for wood and music…I think it turned the old man's head. And every time your brother came back to see him, always carrying some kind of musical instrument, always bringing news of his life…especially after the time that he passed through with the chit he met up in the mountains and was said to have married…it seemed that it turned your father's head a little further. It seemed that he began to hate the forest…and, to be honest, to hate us, for no reason. There was bad blood, Mamzelle, and I can't deny it…."

"It's all right," Catrianne assured her, dishonestly, anxious to hear more facts, if the crone had any more to give. The rest of the group had already drifted away about the business, leaving the burden of further explanation to its sole inheritor.

"Anyway," the old woman went on, "as I said, one day, he abandoned the foundry, which was failing anyway, and disappeared. Nobody knows where he went, and that let out a lot of the bad blood, in spiteful talk: silly talk, mostly. Some said, and still say, that he fled into the wild forest, determined to live like a bear or a wolf—for only bears and wolves, he had once been heard to say while in his cups, know the true joy of unselfconsciousness—but no one knows for sure."

"I can't believe that," murmured Catrianne, distraught.

"Nor me, of a man like that. What is true, though, that before he went, he took a bell that he had cast for the church, in his cart, all the way to the tarn in the dale, and rolled it into the water, saying that it didn't belong in a church, chiming the hours and summoning the devout to prayer, but in the dark water. I doubt that anyone actually heard him say anything, but some said that he shouted out that the spirits of the lake were welcome to roll it back and forth, so that its echoes would toll within our hearts like the knell of doom. Like everybody else, of course, he knew the tale about a founder of bells who went to dwell in the wild forest, among the fae-folk, and that's probably what prompted some to say that he'd done the same himself."

"But you're too sensible to believe that yourself?" Catrianne suggested, a trifle maliciously.

"Of course, Mamzelle. If that really is what he did, he would have perished, but what I think is that, even mad, he would have gone along the road, further inland—not up into the mountains, but along the left fork, all the way to the plain, to the big city, there to start a new life, as far away from the forest as possible. It was the forest he really hated, you see, rather than the people...rather than us."

"I know the story about the bell-founder seduced by the fairies," Catrianne said, pensively, "but it wasn't my father who told it. He hated all talk of the fae-folk, and to him, the notion of a metalworker seduced by them...you're absolutely right, Madame. He would have gone the other way, inland, toward the plain."

"Yes, Mamzelle. Except...."

"Except?"

"Nothing, Mamzelle. I must get this bread home, and so should you."

That seemed to be sound advice to Catrianne, and she followed it. During the short walk home, however, she guessed what the exception that the old woman had suppressed must be. As she had already remarked, what encouraged the conviction of some of the crones that Ernand had gone into the forest was their previous conviction that he had already been seduced once by the fae-folk, by the changeling the latter had foisted on the woodcutter.

Catrianne couldn't help adding an "except" for her own to that. *Except*, she thought, *that even if my mother had been a changeling, she couldn't have had any idea of what she was. She must always have believed herself to be the woodcutter's daughter, and fully human. At the most, a gnome, a goblin or a fay abandoned in a human cradle might have felt a vague sense of difference, of not quite belonging...but that means nothing. I've always felt that, and I'm certainly no changeling...*

am I?

There was no opportunity to flow that train of thought further, because she had to return to practical matters. Handsel and Chanterelle were already up and dressed, and exceedingly hungry. The good bread and fresh milk were devoured with a prodigious appetite by all three of them.

Then Catrianne set off for the church, to see what the curé had to say regarding the ownership of the foundry. It was not the curé she remembered but a younger replacement, who had not been in position long, and had hardly known her less-than-godly father; nevertheless, he knew enough to explain her situation to her with regard to the law, once she had explained her personal situation in the wake of the disaster.

Again, the news was bad.

"I fear that your father did not take the trouble to put his affairs in order before he left," the priest told her. "Quite the reverse, in fact. He was commissioned by the bishop to make a bell for the church, but the project seemed to alarm him once he had undertaken it, for some superstitious reason, and instead of delivering it to me, as he could and should have done, he took it into his head to tip it into a deep pond. There were other derelictions, of whose detail I am unaware, but he left unpaid debts behind. Their total was not great, and he could easily have recovered solvency had he applied himself to it wisely and energetically, but his absence gave his creditors the opportunity to have his property seized, pending sale. The sale would already have gone through had the creditors not fallen to fighting among themselves, with regard to the division of spoils much greater than their moral due. No one in the village will object to your staying there for the time being, and most of them will think, as I do, that you have a moral right to the property, but the law is the law, always there for malevolent men to exploit. I fear that it's only a matter of time before a bailiff appears who will dispossess you—a few months, at the most."

"Thank you," said Catrianne, dully.

"Do you have other relatives in the village? Your mother's family, perhaps."

Catrianne laughed briefly. "No human family," she said. "And if she had another, I doubt that they can care about us."

"I don't know what you mean by that," the curé confessed.

"I suppose not. It isn't the kind of rumor the old women would repeat while displaying their piety. My mother was accused by the superstitious of being a changeling."

"Ah!" said the Churchman. "I do my very best to lead the flock away from such superstitions, but here in the forest…you grew up here, I suppose, and understand."

"I do," Catrianne agreed.

"The Church makes what provision it can for the poor and the dispossessed," the curé told her. "You're not married?"

"No."

"Then you and your niece might well find refuge in a convent. As for the boy, I can search on his behalf for an apprenticeship—not here, obviously, since the village has been dying slowly since the foundry closed, but I can write to my colleagues on his behalf. His woodworking skills, although immature, offer a platform on which to build."

"You're very kind," Catrianne told him, sincerely, if a trifle unenthusiastically. "I need time to think, and to consult the children. I'll come back."

She returned to house adjacent to the Foundry, desolate, and explained to the children what the priest had told her.

"It would give us a breathing-space," she said. "If the curé's connections can find Handsel an apprenticeship, and...."

"No," said Chanterelle, very definitely.

Catrianne tried to embark on an explanation of the fact that even if the little girl were to be placed in the custody of nuns for a while, it would not commit her to taking holy orders when she was older, but she was not given the chance.

"No," said Chanterelle, flatly. "We can't do that."

"We don't have any alternative," Catrianne told her, wearily.

"We have to go into the mountains."

"To look for your mother's family?"

"Yes. That's where we have to go. I know it is."

"But you can't know," Catrianne protested. She turned to Handsel for support, but the support was not forthcoming.

"We have to do as Chanterelle says," he said, firmly.

"You know it too, do you?" snapped Catrianne, almost at the end of her tether.

"No—but I believe that Chanterelle knows. Don't you?"

It was on the tip of Catrianne's tongue to say that not only did she not believe it, but that, as she had just said, it was quite impossible for Chanterelle to know anything of the sort...but suddenly, like a fit of vertigo, she not only lost that conviction, but fell into a well of confusion, no longer certain that she could know better than Chanterelle...or, indeed, that she could know anything at all.

And in any case, she thought, *what is there to lose. In three or four days, we'll be able to set forth again, and it's unlikely to take us that much longer to go from here to the hamlet on the mountain that it took to come from the town to here. The way will be steep, but that means that if we have to come back, it will be downhill all the way. Suppose that Melusine is still alive and well, and only refraining from contact with her daughter for fear of what her supposedly-wicked sister might do if she found out where she is? We have time to look—and if I don't, would they ever forgive me for not trying? Would I ever forgive myself?*

And after all, could I really bear to send the rest of my life in a convent?

After a long pause, she eventually said: "You're right, Chanterelle. We have to explore all our options. The curé will understand that. We have very little money left, but if we eke it out, we can live for a fortnight, perhaps a little more…and if I can remember what I learned as a child, we can find at least some food in the forest. We'll rest for four or five days, and build up our strength, and then we'll go. If we don't find anything, then we'll come back. The people here won't let us starve, while the curé attempts to make what arrangements he can for us."

"We won't come back," said Chanterelle.

"I hope we won't have to," said Catrianne, dully, wishing that she had more psychological fuel for that hope than she actually had.

IX

The High Forest

When Catrianne had explained to the curé what her intentions were, the rumor soon went around that she and the children were going to leave again in order to go further into the highlands, but the local crones, always ready to misinterpret circumstances, settled on the assumption that she was going to look for her father.

"If you find him," more than one of them said, "bring him back." One added: "The village needs him. Without the foundry, it will die. With the forest all round us, we can't grow our own food, and what we can forage there won't nourish the children that the plague has left. Our men can't even become woodcutters and charcoal-burners without the foundry to buy their produce—we're too far away from the markets."

Surprised by the hope they seemed to be investing in her—even more desperate than her own, it seemed—she was carefully not to snuff it out entirely by telling them that she had no intention even of looking for her father. And after all, why should she not enquire after him, as they went along the road, in case he actually had gone that way?"

Honesty, however, compelled her to say. "I fear that our chances finding him are slim. Even if we do, I don't know whether we'll be able to persuade him to come back."

"We understand that," the crones admitted, "but we'll pray that meeting his grandchildren for the first time will persuade him that it's better by far to live as a human than to run wild like a bear or a wolf."

"Will he not have become a werewolf, if he has been away too long?" asked one of the more superstitious, when a group intercepted Chatrianne outside the baker's shop one morning.

"No," said another. "That's not how werewolves are made. But there's a story, is there not, about a boy abandoned in the woods who was raised by wolves, and eventually became their king...."

"No, said a third, "it was a girl-child, adopted by a she-bear, who became the wife of one of her foster-brothers, and became the queen of the bear tribe. She called upon their aid to reclaim her inheritance, and they wreaked a terrible vengeance on her behalf.

"I doubt that my father can be living among wolves or bears," Catrianne told them, "but I know of men who, becoming disenchanted with their lives when they took stock in middle age, retired to remote mountain hamlets in order to study the stars and live in peace. I know of a hamlet high in the mountains...."

"The one where your brother found his wife?" asked one.

"Yes," said Catrianne. "You remember that, then?"

"I remember," said one of the old women, proudly. "He was delivering a musical instrument of an unknown kind, which a wizard had commissioned him to make."

"I remember it too," said another, "but it was a witch, not a wizard, and the witch gave him her daughter in return...." That one fell silent, however, as she glimpsed Catrianne's expression, and realized that further fanciful allegations about Lucinia's suspected ancestry might not be welcome.

"You're right, though, Mamzelle," supplied the old woman who had been her first informant, on the morning after her arrival. "We should have thought of that. Your brother called to see his father on the way out and the way back, a week later, with the mountain girl on the rump of his horse. He must have told him about the hamlet, and what he found there. That might be where his father went. You others, let's pray that Mamzelle finds him there, and brings him back. He'll come, I'm sure, once he sees those two children, and realizes that he's their sole support."

"By all means pray," said Catrianne, with a slight sigh, and went on her way, without bothering to remind them that the foundry no longer belonged to her father, and that even if she were, by some miracle, able to find him and bring him back, he would not simply be able to pick up where he had left off."

At least, however, the inhabitants of the village seemed to be wishing her well, and were not holding the bad blood that her father had engendered against her and the children. All the old crones, in fact, seemed taken with the children, especially Handsel, whom they thought an exceptionally handsome boy.

"The villagers seem to think that we're going in search of my grandfather," Handsel told her, the day before they were due to set off again, having made what preparations they could.

"I never told them that," Catrianne assured him, "but I've let them believe it. In any case, we don't really know exactly what we're looking for, or exactly what we might find when we reach the hamlet. They can't help making up stories, and being desperate in the search for hope. They've lived through the plague, as we have, and have lost loved ones to it."

"I think I would rather find my grandmother than my grandfather," the boy confessed.

"She lives in the forest," Chanterelle put in. "We need to live in the forest. She lives near the secret place, and she can read the dream. If we can find her…" But she trailed off then, perhaps conscious of the magnitude of that *if.*

But it's necessary that we find something, Catrianne thought. *If we come back alone and empty-handed, utterly devoid of resources, it will not matter that the hopes they invested in us were absurd; they will still have been dashed, and their charity will not extend far in that circumstance. We might be reduced, as some of them already seem to be, to foraging in the forest for food.*

When she gave that matter further thought, however, she wondered if it might not be better, if that were to be the case, to remain in the highest part of the forest, where there was evidently a living to be made by foraging, if Lucinia's people really had lived by that means. She had asked Chanterelle for further details of the stories her mother had told her about Alastor's adventure in Melusine's hut, and although the details that the little girl had been able to give her were obviously confused, and very vague, she had certainly formed the impression that the mountain folk got by, albeit frugally, without the assistance of agriculture, and with very limited livestock.

Even if Melusine is dead, she thought, *her hut might still be there, inhabited by some relative who might recognize Handsel and Chanterelle as kin. Even her supposedly evil sister might do that, and might not be as evil as Lucinia reckoned, on the basis of a family quarrel. I know from my childhood experience that the forest is full of food, at this time of year, for those bold enough to risk its hazards. There are nuts, and berries, and mushrooms, which I know how to select in order to avoid poisons.*

As they were leaving, she called in at the church to see the curé one last time, in order to seek his blessing, for what it might be worth. He gave it willingly.

"Commend yourself to the charity of Heaven, my daughter," he said to them. "I am sure that Heaven will not let you down, if you have virtue enough to match your courage. There is a story about a boy named Handsel, as I recall, and his little sister, which ended happily enough—not that I, a priest, can approve of the pagan taint which such stories invariably have. In the final analysis, there is only one true story, and it is the story of our savior."

"That isn't so, sir," said Chanterelle. "There are other true stories."

"You misunderstand me, child," said the priest. "Yes, there are other stories that are true in a trivial sense—but they are trivial. The story of our salvation is the only truly important one."

Catrianne tried to give Chanterelle a surreptitious warning glance, but the little girl was not looking at her.

Fortunately, Chanterelle did not press the point. It was not until they were out on the road again, and out of earshot of the little church that she said to Catrianne. "It's not the only important one to me—or to Handsel and you."

"No," said Catrianne, "it's not. But the priest has his own concerns, and he's a good man. He's the only one here who has offered us real help, and the only one to whom we'll be able to turn if we have to come back. And he might be right about the charity of Heaven, given that all the hymns that you and your mother used to sing must have been heard there, and appreciated. You really ought to sing again, you know. I can still accompany you on the flute I have in my pack."

"Not now," said Chanterelle. "Not here. Not yet."

Catrianne took the final component of the triplet as a sign of encouragement.

Some of the villagers waved goodbye to them as they left the clearing and went into the forest, and Catrianne saluted them, if only to say goodbye.

They had no alternative but to do a certain amount of foraging once they were in the high forest, having taken the fork in the road that led up into the mountain rather than the one that led down toward the plain, because inns were far fewer and further between there that they had been to the east of the village. It was not a route that many people traveled on foot, and those who did generally carried more abundantly-stocked knapsacks than Catrianne and the children were able to do. They routinely moved away from the road, therefore, in order to search for nuts and berries, which were not impossible to find, but not easy either. Trees bearing edible nuts were in a small minority, and although numerous brambles bore ripening berries, they were equipped with ferocious thorns that snagged their clothing and left bloody trails on their hands and arms. Such excursions slowed their progress along the road considerably.

It quickly became obvious, however, that Chanterelle had a natural gift for insinuating herself through the densest undergrowth without mishap, and learned with remarkable rapidity to avoid scratches while picking berries.

There were mushrooms too, but at first the two children were wary of collecting them—even the ones that Catrianne identified as chanterelles. She assured them that they were tasty as well as safe to eat, but they were still hesitant.

"Some mushrooms are poisonous," Handsel said, dubiously. "There are some called death-caps and destroying angels, and I don't know how to tell them apart from the ones that are safe to eat. I heard a story once, which said that some of fae-folk love to squat on the heads of mushrooms, and that although those that the good fays use remain perfectly safe to eat, those favored by goblins become coated with an invisible poisonous slime, so that even ones that seem safe can still be dangerous."

"I can recognize most of those that are safe to eat," Catrianne assured him, "and I think the story about the fae-folk is just a fantasy intended to warn children to be careful."

Chanterelle agreed with her that the story was probably fantastic, but she agreed with Handsel that it might be best to avoid eating mushrooms for the time being.

"As you wish," sad Chatrianne, "but I'll save some for us anyway, for when you're hungrier."

In the event, that did not take long. The bread they had brought from the village only lasted two days, and they soon had no money left to renew the supply on the rare opportunities that presented themselves. Their progress was painfully slow, especially when they left the branch of the main road to follow steeper and more rugged paths, which no cart could follow, and where all goods had to be carried by sure-footed beasts of burden. The further up the mountain they went, the harder the going became, but they were still several leagues short of the hamlet that was their ultimate objective.

Chatrianne did make enquiries about Ernand at a few inns along the way, where she found people who knew the iron-master's name, and even what he looked like, but none had seen him, and several assured her that he could not have passed that way without their knowing.

"You've taken the wrong fork," two of them advised her. "It was necessary to go down to the plain." One of them, however, was conscientious enough to add: "Of course, you wouldn't have any chance of finding him in that vast region, filled with people. If he had come this way, at least you'd have had a chance of picking up his trail."

Chatrianne also asked about a woman named Melusine, but no one had heard of her, although they had heard of a fay by that name featured in an ancient tale of a man whose wife forbade him every to look at her on a certain day of the week, but was eventually conquered by curiosity and saw something terrible through the keyhole of her apartment. Some versions of the story did not specify what he saw, other alleged that the fay-wife was a giant serpent from the waist down, or even the neck down, having been interrupted part way through a periodic metamorphosis."

"That was a very long time ago," of course, one of her informants—

an old woman, inevitably—told her, unnecessarily, "so the woman for whom you're enquiring must simply have been named after the fay. Always an unwise thing to do, to give a child a fay's name, especially in these parts."

"Why in these parts, especially?" Catrianne could not help enquiring.

"Oh, the fae-folk are still active here," she was told, "and malevolent too. Best to avoid catching their attention, even by something as trivial as borrowing a name. What's your little girl's name?"

"Chanterelle," said Catrianne.

The old woman squinted at the child. "Never heard of a fay called Chanterelle," she admitted. "Never head of a girl called after a mushroom either, mind—but at least you didn't call her Amanita." The woman made the sign of the cross.

"Amanita?" Catrianne queried.

"Shh!" said the woman. "Once is enough."

"I don't understand," Catrianne confessed.

"Poisonous mushroom," the woman muttered, sententiously, as if citing a proverb, "poisonous fay."

"You've heard of a fay of that name?"

"Who hasn't?" was the reply she received—although, in fact, Catrianne had only heard Melusine's sister referred to as a witch…but she supposed that the categories inevitably overlapped somewhat in popular understanding and parlance.

The revelation gave her some pause for thought. If people in these parts thought it dangerous to name children after fays, then who would have called two daughters Melusine and Amanita? But she remembered that Lucinia's family had been immigrants from elsewhere, quite probably regarded with suspicion and a degree of hostility simply by virtue of that fact. Perhaps names traditional to their culture had been adopted by the natives as the name of imaginary fays—or perhaps the incomers had adopted the names of the fays of local folklore, as a gesture of defiance or a way of implying that they had special abilities…such as fortune-telling.

The three travelers went on, slowly but inexorably, toward their goal. The children soon became hungry enough to overcome their caution and eat the mushrooms that Catrianne had saved for them, and further ones that she picked on their behalf. They did not eat well, but they did not starve, and they found mountain streams easily enough in which the water seemed clean and not in the least brackish.

The wild forest was not consistent in its nature. Although the lower slopes were hospitable to nut-trees and edible berries, those food-supplies became increasingly sparse as Catrianne and the two children went higher and higher. Their fifth day of foraging took them into a region where many of the trees seemed to be dressed in dark, needle-like leaves and there seemed to be almost nothing to eat except for mushrooms and plants that Catrianne did not recognize, because they were rare or non-existent in the area around the foundry.

It was rare by then, even alongside the path, to find the slightest sign of human habitation, and they all began to wonder whether they had not made a mistake in being so ambitious in their quest. Although the distance between the foundry and the hamlet had not looked much further than the distance between the foundry and the town on the map that Catrianne had consulted, the map had not allowed for changes in altitude, and had caused Catrianne to underestimate the effects of the lateral winding of the path. Measured pace by pace, the distance was considerably further, and the terrain much more difficult.

"Well," said Catrianne, as they settled down to spend yet another night in the forest, bedded down on a mattress of leaf-litter, "I suppose Heaven must be on our side, else we'd have been eaten by wolves or bears before now. If we're to eat at all tomorrow we must trust our luck to guide us to the most nourishing mushrooms and keep us safe from the worst."

"I suppose so," said Handsel, who seemed to have looking closely at all the mushrooms they had passed since leaving the path in search of the means to make a evening meal, perhaps hoping to catch a glimpse of a fay at rest. He had evidently seen none as yet, but that did not seem to make him any more cheerful as they settled down to a frugal repast consisting almost entirely of mushrooms and a few meager nuts, washed down with water from a spring.

"The undergrowth is becoming much thicker hereabouts," Chanterelle pointed out. "There must be many more edible plants than there were in the region through which we've just passed."

"It's a mixed blessing," Catrianne said, with a sigh. It makes foraging much more wearisome—at least for Handsel and me. I don't know how you insinuate yourself through the densest tangles with such agility."

"I'm thin," said the little girl, dismissively.

"I'm not much more than a walking skeleton myself," Chatrianne muttered.

They found it difficult to sleep, and tried for a little while to comfort one another by telling old, familiar stories—but they found the tales comfortless and they slept badly. The mushrooms with which they continued to take the edge off their hunger did not seem to cause their stomachs any considerable upset; but when they fell asleep, they all dreamed, and they all dreamed strangely—strangely enough to want to share the dreams with their companions when they woke up in the morning.

Chanterelle told Catrianne and Handsel that she had dreamed that an old man was chasing her through the forest, determined to make her sing again no matter what the cost. That made Chatrianne shudder, even though she had no reason to think that Chanterelle knew the end of the story about the man who knew the secret of making nightingales sing by day and had eventually applied the method to his ward.

"He didn't catch you, though?" Catrianne said.

"No, he didn't," Chanterelle replied. "Usually, nightmares in which I'm being chased wake me up, but this one didn't."

"What happened, then?" asked Handsel.

"Just as the old man was about to catch me," she told them "a she-wolf jumped on his back and knocked him down—and then set about devouring him while I looked on."

"That must have been horrible," Catrianne observed.

"No, it wasn't. It didn't upset me at all. I just watched, and my heart stopped hammering, slowing down to its normal pace, as the fear I'd felt ebbed away. When the wolf had finished with the bloody mess that had been the old man, she looked at me, and said: 'You needn't be afraid. Broceliande is still alive here, and has no intention of dying. The dream will protect you, if it can, but you might have to change, in order to sing again.'

"I knew then that although I was dreaming, I was also part of the dream—the dream of the forest—and I knew that we were getting close to where we had to go.

"'Are you Melusine?' I asked the she-wolf. The she-wolf said no, but that she had known Melusine for a long time, and that there would be others looking out for us.

"'You are one of the fae-folk though, aren't you?' I asked her.

"'I was,' she said, 'but the dream is changing. The fae-folk aren't what they were. The forest is dying, but death isn't complete, for Broceliande any more than it is for a single tree. Just as the tree can produce seeds, which can give birth to new trees, Broceliande might be able to produce dream-seeds, which can give birth to new dreams. Not all seeds grow, though, and there are predators of dreams, just as there are predators of seeds. Be wary, Chanterelle. Be ready to run, if you have to—leave Catrianne and Handsel behind, if you must.'

"That wasn't all, but I can't remember the rest. That was the message, what the dream wanted to tell me. What did it tell you?"

"It wasn't really a message, Chanterelle," said Catrianne, a trifle uneasily. "It was just a dream."

"No," said Chanterelle. "If it had only been a dream, the she-wolf wouldn't have spoken to me in the secret language. But perhaps you didn't have true dreams, because you don't know the secret language, do you?"

At a loss to know what to say, Catrianne said nothing, for the moment.

"I dreamed about a wolf too," said Handsel, "but I don't know whether it was a she-wolf. I thought it was a werewolf, though, and I was afraid when I saw it creeping up on me, in case it bit me and I became a werewolf too. It seemed to know that I'd thought that—which isn't really surprising, I suppose, as it was in my dream and in my head, where thoughts can't really be private. It spoke to me, like your wolf, but in ordinary language.

'You shouldn't be afraid,' it said to me. 'There's really no need. It's not so bad, being a werewolf, because your grandfather was wrong to think he'd find the dubious solace of unconsciousness in the world of bears and wolves. If you decide to become a werecreature, you'll be more conscious than before. You don't have to be bitten, either. All you have to do is choose the right dream.'

"I've heard too many stories, though, in which wolves are deceivers, trying to lure innocents into traps. They're not as cunning as foxes, it's said but I was still wary. I didn't want to let the wolf know that I didn't trust it, though, so I nodded my head slowly, as if I were promising to think about it. I think it knew what I was really thinking, through, because it barked in an odd fashion, that might have been a kind of laugh, before it sidled away.

"Then the forest grew very dark, but I could see a light in the distance: a pale white light. I wanted to go toward it, to see what it was, but I realized then that I was on my own, and I thought that I ought not to go without you. I thought you had to be nearby, and that the only reason I couldn't see you as because it was dark, so I began searching with my hands, but I couldn't find you. I think I searched for a long time, and when I looked again, the white light had gone.

"I remember thinking that I wished that I were more conscious, as the wolf had promised that I might be, if I weren't stuck so obstinately in my human form, but I didn't want to let go of who and what I am, because…well, because it's who and what I am. And some time after that, I woke up, with that thought still buzzing in my head, as if it were important. But you're right, Aunt Cat—it was just a dream. It doesn't really mean anything, does it?"

"Probably not," said Catrianne, uncertainly.

"But what did you dream Aunt Cat?" asked Chanterelle, swiftly. "You did dream, didn't you? Did you see a wolf too?"

"No," said Catrianne. "I...." She stopped.

"You need to tell us, Aunt Cat," said Chanterelle, seriously. "Even if they are just dreams, that doesn't mean that they don't mean anything. If this part of the forest really is still dreaming, in the way that the whole forest used to do...well, dreams might be more important here than what happens while we're awake."

Catrianne shrugged her shoulders. "All right," she said. "I dreamed about the kithara. But that's not really surprising, is it?"

"The kithara?" repeated Handsel, puzzled.

"The musical instrument that your father came up here to deliver. I was the first person to play it—really play music on it, that is, rather than just plucking the strings one by one to see whether they were in tune, and sampling chords to check that they rang true. At first, obviously, it was strange, and I had no idea how to get a tune out of it, but I soon figured at out.

"My dream started out with remembering that—I remembered picking up the instrument, and cradling it, then getting the feel of it. But when I first played it, more than thirteen years ago, I picked out a tune that I knew, something that I'd played on other, simpler lyres. In my dream last night I played different music—music I'd never hard before."

"Music written on trees?" asked Chanterelle.

"No, it wasn't written anywhere. I was making it up as I went... except that I wasn't, really. It was...as if it were already in the kithara, and I was only bringing it out. And there was an accompaniment, but I honestly don't know whether the other instrument, or voice, was a flute of some kind, or birds, or even a human voice modulated like birdsong or the notes of a flute. I couldn't see anyone, or anything. I was still in the forest, I think, but I couldn't see any trees: just mist. Silvery mist... like a cloud, or...."

"Or what," Handsel prompted.

"I don't know. Like...gaseous music, or like disorganized matter, not even gaseous, but ethereal, but somehow possessed, not of life, but of rhythm, perhaps even melody. In fact, I had the sensation that perhaps I was part of the music I was playing, that my body was only a kind of phantom, a visual appearance...but that doesn't make sense, because I was certainly solid enough to hold the kithara, and to play it."

"I hadn't thought about that," said Chanterelle, quietly.

"About what?" Handel asked.

"About the music, the song of the dream."

"There was singing in your dream too?"

"No, no, not this time…not yet…not singing *in* the dream, the song *of* the dream."

"I don't understand what you mean," Handsel complained."

"Nor do I," whispered Chanterelle—but Catrianne was deeply impressed by the strange expression on the little girl's face: an expression of fervent concentration, as if she were trying with al the might of her immature, eleven-year-old mind, to understand something still beyond it, not because she was too young, but because she had not found the exotic direction in which her imagination and her reason needed to go, in order to reach that understanding.

"Too many mushrooms," opined Catrianne. "I suppose we should be grateful that they didn't make us sick, or give us indigestion, but they must be giving us strange dreams."

"Yes," Handsel agreed. "But there's nothing much else to eat hereabouts, is there?"

X

The Cabin

Even while making that observation, Handsel was already busy, and he had soon gathered more white and orange mushrooms, which he offered to his companions for breakfast. He seemed fitter than he had been the previous day, and he was noticeably more cheerful than before, so it seemed to Catrianne that sleep, and perhaps even his dream, must have done him good. Chanterelle was still very pensive, as if still partly becalmed in her dream, but she too seemed physically energized, and ready for another stage in their interminably journey.

After eating a few mushrooms each, and drinking from the stream, the three of them made their way back to the nearby path, and continued to make their way along it, trying to stride purposively although their feet were very sore. They sky was cloudy, and seemed to be threatening rain. The peak of the mountain was shrouded by cloud, but the rain held off as they trudged up the path.

Catrianne, bringing up the rear of the little group, had just settled into a semi-automatic stride, when they reached a bend, and Chanterelle, who was immediately in front of her, stopped dead, almost causing her to knock her down and fall over her.

The little girl pointed, and said: "We're here."

The path curved to the right because there was an outcrop of rock that it steered around, and nestling within the aggregation of rocks, whose surfaces had been smoothed by centuries of rain, there was a fissure about the height of a man, wide enough and deep enough for a man to wedge himself into it, along with a knapsack, but no wider, and hardly any deeper.

"What do you mean?" Catrianne asked.

"That's the gap in which Father took shelter the night of the storm."

"How do you know?" asked Handsel, who had taken a few further steps forward but now turned round and came back.

"I know," said Chanterelle. "Mother's story described it, in the secret language. There's no mistake. That's the place where he sheltered from the rain, with the kithara."

"Well, so what?" said Handsel. "It isn't raining yet, and even if it were, the three of us wouldn't all fit in there."

Without deigning to reply, Chanterelle went to stand in the cleft in the rock, adjusting her position, carefully, and standing on tiptoe in order to make herself taller.

"I'm not big enough," she said, in a tone of annoyance. "Come and lift me up, Aunt Cat."

Catrianne suppressed the impulse to ask why, and simply did as she was asked, lifting the girl up so that her head was a higher than her own.

"That's right," said Chanterelle. "That's exactly right. That's the direction. Mark it carefully, so we don't go wrong." She pointed into the trees on the opposite side of the road, which seemed uncommonly densely packed, and unusually varied, for the altitude that they had now reached.

"What are you talking about?" Handsel asked.

"That's where Father saw the light," said Chanterelle. "That's where Melusine's cabin is."

"Are you sure, darling?" Catrianne asked her.

"Yes," Chanterelle replied, with total confidence. "But you'll have to let me lead the way. I can get through, I know I can. You'll lose your way if you don't stay close behind me—Handsel first, and then you, Aunt Cat. Don't lose sight of me for an instant. It's only fifty paces, if you walk with the dream, but if you sidestep…you'll have to be careful, that's all."

Catrianne set her down, and Chanterelle crossed the path. The undergrowth seemed to the naked eye to be too dense for such a small and frail person to shove her way into it, but Chanterelle did not seem to shove at all. Instead, she insinuated herself into the screen of foliage. It was Catrianne who had to shove Handsel after her, to make sure that he did not lose sight of her, and then to follow in her turn.

Chanterelle seemed so utterly sure of herself that Catrianne could not bring herself to doubt that Melusine's cabin really was there, or that Chanterelle could find it. She had no sooner begun to think that it would be easy, however, than it suddenly became exceedingly problematic.

For five days and more they had left the path at intervals to go into the forest without catching sight of any predator, or any sizeable animals at all, except for the occasional glimpse of a fleeing roe deer. They had sometimes heard the rustling of small mammals that they had not actually seen, but which Catrianne had assumed to be mice, rats and hedgehogs, perhaps pursued by the occasional weasel, but they had not been troubled by any of them.

Now, however, Chanterelle had scarcely taken ten confident paces into the dense verdure, followed by Handsel and Catrianne, than they were suddenly confronted by a bear, which immediately reared up on its hind legs, seemingly as surprised by the encounter as they were.

It was not a huge bear, only a little taller when upright than Catrianne, and its thinning coat was showing distinct traces of mange, but it was a great deal broader and burlier than Catrianne, let alone poor Chanterelle, who seemed almost to be within paw's reach. Catrianne could not help the alarming thought that its seeming ill-health might induce it to be all the more anxious to make a meal of them.

It did not reach out aggressively in their direction with its clawed forepaw, however. It simply remained still, balanced on its hind legs, staring at them curiously. Then it sneezed, and used its right forepaw to wipe its muzzle, in a fashion that seemed almost apologetic. Its lips curled back, showing racks of yellow teeth, but the gesture did not seem menacing; it was more akin to a wry smile.

Had Catrianne been on her own, she would have turned and run away, as fast as she could go, but she could not do that while Handsel and Chanterelle were there, in front of her, and there was no way that she could somehow pull them past her and shove them in the direction of the road. Handsel backed up slightly, his body making contact with hers, but Chanterelle did not move a muscle, seeming more content on holding her direction than protecting her frail body from any assault by the monster.

"It's all right," said Chanterelle to the bear, in a tone that was apprehensive, but resolute. "It's only me. I'm going to my grandmother's cabin. If you've been set to guard it, it isn't from me."

The bear stroked its puzzle with its paw again, and looked even more puzzled than before. Then it leaned forward. Catrianne was a head taller than Handsel, who was a head taller than Chanterelle. As the bear inspected all three of them, therefore, Catrianne was able to meet its eyes, and feel its fetid breath on her face, at a distance that could not have been more than half a dozen handspans.

"It's all right," Chanterelle said "Catrianne is my father's sister. We're entitled to be here."

The bear still seemed profoundly uncertain—and, it seemed to Catrianne, profoundly stupid. She could not believe for an instant that it could understand what Chanterelle was saying to it, which was phrased in ordinary terminology, not in any kind of magical secret language.

Handsel suddenly bent down, and picked up something from the ground—two things, in fact, one with each hand. One was a pine-cone, the other a small stone. As weapons went, they left a great deal to be desired, and Catrianne reached out to stop him throwing them, convinced that he could only irritate the beast, and might provoke the attack that it was—but he simply shrugged off the hand with which she tried to restrain him, and threw the pine-cone from his right hand before transferring the stone to the same hand so that her could follow it up immediately.

The pine-cone hit the bear on the nose, and the stone bounced off its furry forehead, quite harmlessly.

The bear moved its head back, startled but not hurt, and then looked Handsel in the eyes with utter disdain.

Chanterelle jabbed her elbow backwards into Hansel's midriff with such force that he gasped. Perhaps that prevented him from bending down to pick up more ineffectual missiles, but Catrianne guessed that he had simply realized the utter impotence of the gesture.

Then the bear looked down at Chanterelle again.

Catrianne thought for a split second that the bear actually bowed to her, but then concluded that it was merely settling back on to four feet, becoming a quadruped again. Having done that, it turned round—surprisingly, given the lack of space ceded by the tangled vegetation—and moved away, disappearing behind the green curtain in a matter of seconds.

"Either it wasn't hungry enough," Catrianne whispered, hoarsely, unable to raise her voice any further, "or you actually tamed it, darling."

"No," said Chanterelle, "it's a good sign. If the cabin is guarded, there must be something to guard."

The girl paused in order to get her breath back, and Catrianne realized that she must have been badly frightened, in spite of her apparent composure, but she did not take her long to pull herself together.

"Let's go," she said. "Stay close."

So saying, she took another step forward, and then another—but then it seemed that she must have put her foot into a hole hidden beneath foliage, because her body suddenly titled sideways, and she stumbled. She yelped in pain, but immediately tried to adjust her posture, while holding her position. She had evidently twisted her ankle, though, and paused again, hesitating to put her weight on it.

"Don't move," she said, immediately. "It'll be all right in a minute. It doesn't hurt—no worse than before, anyway. Just hold still."

"What if the bear comes back?" Handsel asked, hoarsely indeed. "I frightened it, but if it's hungry enough…."

Chanterelle jabbed him in the ribs again with her sharp elbow.

"What's that for?" he complained.

"Don't let it get to you," she said. "I think it's an imp of some kind, but it probably doesn't have any evil intention—it's just what it does. Put your hands on my shoulders, and give me a minute. We can't be more than a couple of minutes away from the cabin."

"I can't see anything," Catrianne observed.

"You won't," said Chanterelle. "It's hidden, but I know where it is. Just be patient, and I'll take you straight to it. Give me a couple of minutes, and I'll be fine."

"If there's someone there," Handsel suggested, "We could shout, and they might come to meet us."

"Don't do that, please," said Chanterelle.

"If you ankle hurts, darling," said Catrianne, "I can carry you."

"No you can't," said Chanterelle impatiently. "Why won't you understand? The dream guided Father through, but that was thirteen years ago. It's more confused now…and as the she-wolf said, there are predators of dreams. The forest is dying; it's weak."

"Jut a second," said Handsel, and took a sidestep, before Chatrianne could stop him—but Chanterelle had whipped round and grabbed him round the waist.

"Please, Handsel," she begged, apparently not angry with him, "don't listen to the imp, and *don't move*."

It's all right," the brother said, letting his knees buckle, so that he bent down again, as he had when picking up the pine-cone and the stone, without moving his feet from the path that Chanterelle was trying to fray through what Catrianne was now perfectly convinced was no ordinary undergrowth. "I think I can reach it."

"Don't pick it up!" said Chanterelle, obviously without being able to see what *it* might be. Almost immediately, however, realizing that she was too late she amended the instruction to: "Throw it away."

Handel did not throw it away.

"This is odd," he said, holding up the object that he had fished out of the undergrowth so that Catrianne could see it."

It was a small wooden tube, hollowed out and punctured with holes, with a sculpted mouthpiece: a primitive flute.

"It's very crude," he murmured. "It couldn't have been hollowed out with a metal tool, but the finger-holes are very neat. Is it grandmother's, do you think—or perhaps even mother's? It's very old."

He put it to his mouth, evidently to see whether it still worked. It did. Semi-automatically, he sounded the notes of a simple tune that his father had always used to test the musical instruments he made.

"Don't!" said Chanterelle, again too late.

"It's all right," Handsel asued her. "It's just a glorified whistle. He played the sequence of notes again—and something in the forest responded.

Handsel laughed. "That's strange!" he said. "The local birds already know that tune!"

"Please stop," said Chanterelle. "Put it away in your pouch. We need to reach the cabin."

"If there's anyone in there," Handsel said, "either they didn't hear the tune, or thought it was just a bird. I'll try again. Sing along, if you want."

So saying, Handsel put the little pipe to his lips, and blew into it again. He had no difficulty at all producing a different and more complex tune, but it was very faint, and very high-pitched. It was no louder than the voices in which they were speaking, and seemed hardly likely to attract any attention from the invisible cabin, let alone tempt anyone to sing."

"It's a fay flute," said Chanterelle, anxiously. "Put it away, Handsel. You now full well that the stories warn humans to beware of playing elfin music, lest they be captured by the fae-folk."

Handsel inspected the pipe. "I could easily have made it myself," he observed. "Smaller hands than mine might have made it just as easily, I suppose."

"Elfin music loosens the bonds of time, in the tales that mother used to tell," said Chanterelle, uneasily, "and I've heard it said that time untied has weight for no man...."

"Whatever that's supposed to mean," said Handsel.

"I think it means that while a fay flute plays a single song, years might pass in villages and towns," said Chanterelle, faintly. "Oh, what have you done, Handsel? I told you not to listen to the imp."

"I only wanted to help you sing, Chanterelle—but you might be right about the time. It seems to me that dusk is falling, although it's surely too early, and the darkness under the canopy is deepening. We couldn't see a bear in the dark. If the bear comes back, it'll gobble us all up. Are you sure you can't sing, Chanterelle even if I play you one of your favorite tunes?"

"Even if you could play the song of the dream itself, my dear Handsel," Chanterelle told him, "I couldn't sing a note. Even if you were to do what the man in the story did...."

Catrianne felt obliged to intervene at that point, no matter how far out of her imaginative depth she was.

"Put the pipe away, Handsel," she said, bringing all her adult authority to bear, "or we'll be standing here forever. Can you walk, Chanterelle?"

"Yes," said Chanterelle,

"Can you still find this cabin?"

"Yes."

"Then do it—and Handsel, behave yourself. Do exactly what Chanterelle tells you. We need to get into the cabin before it gets dark or it starts to rain."

Before she had finished the sentence, the rain that had long been threatening began to fall, making a terrible clatter in the forest canopy, although the density of the foliage protected them from the downpour, and only a few stray drops reached them. The dusk thickened, but the darkness was not yet absolute.

"Put your hand on my shoulder, Handsel," Chanterelle ordered, "and you, Aunt Cat, put your hand on Handsel's shoulder, and don't let go."

They both obeyed, and Chanterelle immediately resumed her course through the dense undergrowth, moving with seeming ease in spite of its seeming impenetrability and a slight additional limp caused by her trip.

No further obstacles impeded her progress, and before they had taken three strides Catrianne saw a white light shining through the trees, directly ahead of them. That reassured her enormously, although it did not give the impression of being a lamplit window, and seemed to grow dimmer rather than brighter as they approached it.

Chanterelle was absolutely right, however. There was a building of some kind there, and she really had headed straight toward it, unerringly, since leaving the path.

Hope blossomed in Catrianne's breast. Not merely was there a cabin, but an inhabited cabin. No matter how unlikely it had seemed when they set off from the foundry, and no matter how arduous the journey had been, they had succeeded. They had reached their objective, and found help.

Chanterelle paused at the door of the cabin, and made as if to push it, but Catrianne said: "Wait, darling." She moved Handsel to one side and stepped between him and Chanterelle. She reached out and rapped with her knuckles.

There was a sound of footsteps within, and the door swung inwardly, smoothly and soundlessly.

A dark-haired woman appeared in the doorway, seemingly young—younger than Catrianne. Even in the gloom, Catrianne could see that she was beautiful. She could also judge something of the changing expression on the woman's face. At first, Catrianne thought, the expression had been hopeful, ready to react joyfully to the sight she expected to behold—but as the woman looked her straight in the face, that expression became uncertain. The gaze flickered sideways, left and right, to take in the children before returning immediately to stare at Chatrianne's features, which must have been difficult to discern clearly in the somber twilight, given that the light within the cabin seemed to be even fainter than candlelight, and paler.

"Lucinia?" queried the woman, uncertainly.

"Melusine?" queried Catrianne, with an equal absence of conviction.

Each of them, evidently jumping to the conclusion that their guesses had been mistaken, fell silent momentarily, in confusion.

It was the woman who had opened the door who took the initiative of breaking the silence.

"Melusine isn't here, I'm afraid," said the woman, in a soft and musical voice, leaning forward slightly to peer into the gloom. "In fact, if you have news of her, I'd be extremely glad to hear it. I'm her sister, Amanita."

XI

Amanita

When the stunned silence had stretched to nearly half a minute, Amanita spoke again.

"I see that my reputation has gone before me. Perhaps you've been to the hamlet, where everyone is convinced that I'm a witch who holds regular communion with Satan, or an evil fay. If I were a spell-caster, I dare say that I might cast a few nasty ones in their direction, to pay them back for all their slanders, but the tales they tell exaggerate everything. There really is no need to be afraid. No one who has cause to be afraid of me could ever have found this place. But I don't know you at all, and I find that strange. Would you mind telling me who you are, and how you know Melusine?"

Catrianne assumed that the burden of explanation was hers. She was momentarily tempted, in view of the fact that the other's reputation had indeed gone before her, to lie about her own identity, but she had no idea whether she could do so credibly, so she decided on the truth.

"My name is Catrianne Ernand…." She began.

Amanita had seemed quite composed, but at that statement she started, visibly astonished. There was nothing hostile about her reaction, though. When she spoke, her tone was surprised, but not in the least aggressive.

"Ernand?" she said. "You're related to Alastor Ernand—the woodworker?"

"I'm his sister," said Catrianne, and added, quasi-automatically: "And these are his children, Handsel and Chanterelle."

Amanita immediately knelt down to bring herself down to the children's level. The diminution of her silhouette allowed a little more pale light to emerge from the interior of the cabin and illuminate the children's faces. The alleged witch stared at them intently. Catrianne could no longer read the expression on her beautiful face, but she seemed direly puzzled, and very pensive. Her voice, however, remained silky and smooth, musical and seductive.

"What a handsome boy you are, Handsel!" she said. "I haven't had the pleasure of meeting your father, although we've had some correspondence, but he must be a very handsome man, to have a son like you. And you, my dear," she continued, turning to Chanterelle, "are beautiful, truly beautiful. And what a lovely name. It has something in common with mine, but as you're Alastor Ernand's daughter, I expect he had the musical string in mind. Can you sing, my darling?"

Chanterelle looked her straight in the eyes, and said: "No."

Catrianne knew that it was not a lie, but she also knew that it was a truth deliberately intended to deceive.

"That's a shame," said Amanita. "I've organized the local children into a little choir, and I would love to have had you join it. I call them my nightingales."

That sent a frisson down Catrianne's back, although it appeared to be said in all innocence.

"And where is your father, pray?" Amanita went on, addressing Handsel but looking out into the gloom. "Not wandering out there is the dark, I hope?"

"No," murmured Handsel, deeply embarrassed. "He's dead."

"Dead!" echoed Amanita, seemed once again to be amazed, but she went on, swiftly. "It's raining, though! You must be cold. Come in, come in. The stove isn't lit, I fear, and the furniture is sparse, but there's a couch and two armchairs. Sit down, sit down...."

She ushered them all inside as she spoke. The gloom inside the cabin was almost as crepuscular as the grayness outside, and Catrianne could not make out exactly where the wan light was coming from, but she could distinguish a divan of sorts and the two armchairs that Amanita had indicated. She picked Chanterelle up and deposited her in one of the chairs, immediately turning her attention to the child's ankle. Handsel sat down on the divan.

"Is there something wrong with the child's foot?" Amanita asked.

"She stumbled in the undergrowth," Catrianne explained, "and we all have bad blisters." She had removed Chanterelle's shoe, and noted with alarm as she palpated the ankle that it seemed swollen.

"It's all right," Chanterelle said.

"May I look?" Amanita asked.

Catrianne hesitated. "You've heard that I'm an evil witch who steals children's souls," Amanita said, with a sigh. "Please believe that you're not in the slightest danger. The last thing I would want to do is harm any of you, but I do have some healing skills. Please let me look."

Catrianne moved aside, and Amanita took her place, inspecting and palpating Chanterelle's ankle.

"You're right," Amanita declared. "It's just a slight twist. But your foot is very sore—you must have walked a long way. Surely you haven't walked all the way from the iron-master's foundry?" She turned to Chatrianne. "Please sit down," she added.

Catrianne sat down in the second armchair, and added: "Further than that, I fear."

Amanita stood up again, and moved to a position in which she could see all three of them simultaneously. "I wish I could offer you some food and drink," she said, "but I don't live here. I come here regularly, though, in case Melusine or Lucinia has returned. I've been without news of them for a long time, and I fear...but you have troubles of your own, that's evident. I'm truly sorry to hear about Alastor. When did he die?"

"He died of the plague, nearly two months ago," Catrianne told her.

"Two months ago! I was too late, then? He never received my letter?"

It was Catrianne's turn to be amazed. "Letter?" she queried.

"Yes—a letter commissioning him to make a musical instrument...a special instrument. He made one for me once before, a long time ago. He was a little late with the delivery, but it was such a fine instrument that...." She broke off abruptly, and looked Catrianne in the eyes. "But in that case, how do you come to be here? And why, if you're Alastor Ernand's sister, did you ask for Melusine?"

Then, before Catrianne could begin a reply, Amanita's expression changed again, more drastically than before. This time, there was annoyance mingled with the amazement, and distress with the dawn of enlightenment. "Oh, what a fool I am!" she exclaimed. "What a fool I've been...all these years!"

She knelt down again, and looked at Handsel. "Tell me, handsome boy—your mother's name is Lucinia, is it not?"

"It was," croaked Handsel.

"Was!" This time the dark-haired woman's voice was positively agonized. "Not Lucinia too! What a catastrophe! For thirteen years I've been searching for my niece, and now I finally have news of her it's to hear that she's dead!" She turned to Catrianne. "The plague again?"

"Yes." Catrianne confirmed.

"Oh, the poor thing, the poor thing! Why did she do it? Melusine... and how on earth did she contrive it...?" She caught herself up, paused and then continued: "But I see...I see....you've come here in search of your grandmother. You've been to the forge and found the iron-master gone. So you came here. On foot! You poor, poor things! But this is dreadful! I'm so glad that I happened to be here, although I can't imagine how you found...oh, no! Yes, I *can* imagine, now, how you found the cabin. Perhaps not so dreadful after all, then...."

Again, she paused to think, obviously overwhelmed by so much information that was new to her. She stood up, and moved restlessly around the cramped interior of the cabin.

"You must be terribly sore and weary," she went on, eventually. "I think I can see it all, now...but it's a great deal to take in all at once. What a fool I've been, for all these years! And yet...perhaps it might still work out, if not for the best, at least...but poor Lucinia! If only she'd entrusted herself to me. But Melusine is...perhaps was...her mother, and a child cannot help but love her mother, no matter how foolish she might be...."

She looked at the children, alternately. Her gaze eventually settled on Chanterelle, and she knelt down again before her.

"It was you, my darling, wasn't it, who guided you all here? You were the one who found the cabin...but what must you think of me, child? What must you think of me! You love your mother, undoubtedly, as you certainly should, for she was the most lovable person I ever knew...but she has told you, has she not, that I am wicked? She has instructed you to hate me...or, at the very least, to fear me, and on no account to trust me. That's true isn't it?"

"Yes," said Chanterelle, as frankly and as confidently as she had faced down the bear.

"That's unfortunate...very unfortunate," said Amanita. "And if you've heard my name spoken elsewhere in these parts, it has doubtless only served to deepen the impression...."

She straightened up, and looked at Catrianne. "I don't know you, Mademoiselle," she said, "or these children, and I assume that you must all think very badly of me. I can only ask you to reserve your judgment for a little while, and not to rely too greatly on prejudice. My sister and I have never seen eye to eye; we have had deep differences, and terrible quarrels. Inevitably, Lucinia took her side, and Melusine became even more hostile to me when I tried to persuade her daughter that I was not as black as I was painted. I can't imagine what Lucinia might have told you, but I know that you must be far more frightened of me than the poor peasants hereabouts, who take me for a witch. Perhaps you will not be able to believe me, but I feel the necessity nevertheless to swear to you, on everything that I hold sacred, that the last thing I would want to do is harm any of you.

"These children might be he only relatives I have left in the world if, as I am increasingly beginning to fear, some misfortune has overtaken Melusine. They are my blood, as she is, and I swear to you that no matter how terrible our differences have been I would never, under any circumstances, hurt my sister, her child or her grandchildren. And you are the sister of my grandchildren's father…a craftsman for whom I have…had…the greatest respect. I wish you could believe me, my dear Catrianne, no matter how difficult it might seem, when I tell you that you have absolutely nothing to fear from me, and that if you have come here in search of help, I shall be only to glad to provide all that I can. We are very nearly the last of our kind, my dear, and it is time to put all the old differences away. We are under siege and under threat, and this is no time to be for us to be at odds."

"We?" Catrianne queried. "What, exactly, do you man by *our kind*, Mademoiselle?"

Amanita stared at her, as if trying to read her thoughts.

"Ah!" she said, finally. "She never told him, did she? And she swore Lucinia to secrecy too. What a mania my sister had for secrecy! Yes…yes, I see now. You don't know." Yet again, she knelt down, and stared into Chanterelle's eyes. "But *you* know, child, don't you? You've guessed…or dreamed it. You know. Oh, this is too bizarre!"

Suddenly, she switched her attention to Handsel. "Did your mother ever tell you, handsome boy, how precious you are?"

"All the time," said Handsel, blushing.

Amanita smiled. "But she never told you why, did she? She—Melusine, that is—must have had a plan. She must have had a plan…but it's all gone wrong! Poor Lucinia dead, and Alastor too…and all of you are here. What an inspiration it was to pay my regular visit to her cabin tonight…but no, not an inspiration. The dream brought me! I come once a month, you know, to look for evidence of Melusine having returned, but today…yes, this is no coincidence. Thirteen years! Trivial, in the old days, but not now…not with the threat of world's end suspended above us. And now this…or can this possibly be part of Melusine's plan? Does she know you're here?"

She was talking more to herself than her notional listeners, while deep in hectic thought, and her eyes were flicking from each of her three visitors to the others with unsteady rapidity—but Chanterelle answered one of her questions, calmly, as if it had been addressed to her: "Yes."

Amanita interrupted herself. "What? What's that you say? Melusine knows that you're here? *Here? Now?* Are you sure."

"No," said Chanterelle, still gazing at Amanita as she had gazed at the bear. "I don't know that—but it is part of a plan. Mother always wanted me to come here. There's something I need to do here."

Catrianne was surprised that Amanita did not ask Chanterelle why she thought that, or how she could possibly know it, because she had no idea herself—but Amanita apparently knew more than one thing about Lucinia's daughter that she did not, and paused again, apparently to think about what it might be that Lucinia had wanted Chanterelle to do here. "You haven't answered my question," Catrianne said to Amanita, trying hard to match Chanterelle's serenity.

Amanita turned to meet her gaze. "No," she admitted, "I haven't. But if Melusine has kept it quiet for thirteen years…and she must have guessed, if Alastor found the cabin…which means that she saw the kithara, and that Alastor probably played it for her, or for Lucinia…."

She stopped, but continued almost immediately, having evidently come to a decision. "Yes, my dear Catrianne, I'll tell you everything that Melusine would not, so that you can judge which of us is the honest dealer. I'll tell you everything…but not here. We can't stay here. We must go to my house. You couldn't stay here anyway, the three of you. Look at the place! It isn't a fit residence for children. At my house there's food, and light, and….the kithara. You play, don't you? You've actually played the kithara? Oh, I think I see…I think I'm beginning to understand why the dream brought you…brought us all. But at least you must be sure by now that I'm not a terrible witch…or even a competent dream-reader, else I surely could not have been fooled by my dear sister for all these years, like some stupid human."

"Human?" queried Catrianne, although she already had a hollow feeling in the pit of her stomach, having more than a suspicion of the truth. "You're not human?"

"Of course not," said the fay. "You're only half human yourself—and as for these dear children…do you have the slightest inkling, now, Catrianne, of how precious my darling Handsel might be?"

Catrianne was stunned, incapable of speech.

"No, you don't," concluded Amanita. "Well, I'll explain everything. *Everything*…and then you can make up your minds exactly how wicked I am, and whether you want to join forces with me, in Melusine's inexplicable absence. But we have to go now."

And without another word, she bent over, plucked Chanterelle from the ground, and cradled her in her arms.

Chanterelle struggled momentarily, as if by virtue of a reflex action, but she abandoned the attempt to escape almost immediately.

"Follow me," said the fay magisterially, and strode past Catrianne and through the door of the ill-lit cabin, into the darkness of the night, and the pouring rain.

Before Amanita stepped out of the cabin it was pitch dark outside, but as soon as she crossed the threshold there was light, of a sort. It was not daylight, but a modified gloom similar to the semi-darkness that had reigned inside the cabin. Whatever was producing the faint white light was not aggregated into any kind of obvious source, but there was a diffuse light around them, sufficient for Amanita to steer a course through the forest—a task made easier, in any case, because the forest put up not the slightest resistance to her passage, nor to the passage of her followers, while they were careful to form a kind of retinue. She did not give any order to that effect, as Chanterelle had when they left the path in order to move into the equivocal forest, but Handsel fell into step behind her very meekly, and Catrianne had adapted well enough by now to the apparent order of the strange environment to have figured out what was required of her.

As for Chanterelle, lying in Amanita's arms, not required to make any effort of her own, she tried with all her might to go to sleep. She wanted to dream, because she felt direly in need of guidance, and thought that in this place, perhaps even more so in those arms than lying on the ground on a bed of vegetation, she might be able to dream significantly, if not of the she-wolf then of some other entity capable of giving her advice.

"That's right," my darling, "Amanita whispered in her ear. "Relax. Sleep, if you can. You're safe now. Nothing can hurt you now."

Whether it was suspicion of the fay or some other cause, however, Chanterelle could not relax. Indeed, hunger, which had only been a dull ache before, so everpresent that it had become easy to disregard, was now gnawing at her stomach, so painfully that she could easily have imagined that a phantom bear was clawing at her midriff. She tried to fight the pain, but the only way she could find to do that was to call up a tune within her head and when she did that she could not help imagining a player: Handsel, who was playing the tune on the wooden pipe that had somehow been left for him to find between the path and the cabin.

It was an old tune, perfectly familiar, which she often had heard her father pick out, in his relatively clumsy fashion, on various wind instruments, when testing them, but Chanterelle had never heard it played in such a high register. She wondered whether it might be the key in which a tune was played that made it into elfin music, rather than the tune itself.

At first, when the tune went round and round and round in her sleepless mind there was nothing but the sound of the pipe to be "heard", but as it went on and on it was gradually joined by a chirping avian voice: a voice that was not that of a nightingale, although she could not tell what kind of bird it was, or whether it really was a bird, or whether it might be someone, fay or human, merely imitating a bird.

As Amanita strode through the wood, however, Chanterelle eventually realized that, although the sound of the pipe was in her head, conjured up by her own imagination, the voice of the bird or simulacrum of a bird was not. The voice was real, growing in strength because the singer was growing closer—but how could it be, she wondered, that the imaginary pipe and the real voice were keeping such perfect harmony?

"Don't be distracted by the bird, my darling," Amanita whispered to her. "I have what's needed to drive her away."

Chanterelle raised her head and tried to peer into the faint light, to see whether she could catch a glimpse of the singer. She could not see anything in the crowns of the trees, and was not even sure that the voice was coming from above, but she was suddenly struck by the manner of Amanita's dress. When she answered the knock on the cabin door, she had pulled her cloak about her, and because she had been silhouetted by the light inside the cabin she had given the impression of being clad in black, a creature potentially capable of hiding in shadow. Now, however, the cloak was floating far more loosely, and it was evident that she was wearing a long white dress beneath it, and that the cloak itself was topped by curious cape made from blood-red fur, flecked with black sequins. She also had two dogs with her now, walking to either side of her, cleaving through the undergrowth with the same ease as her, gliding rather than walking. They were like no dogs Chanterelle had seen before; they were lean and white, like huge spectral greyhounds, with a stride so capacious that they could surely have out-sprinted any greyhound in the world.

"Go, Verna, Virosa," said the fay. "Chase that annoying bird away."

The dogs, obediently, slipped away—and immediately, the birdsong, real or imitation, began to fade away into the distance. The sound of the pipe faded with it, even though that was entirely in Chanterelle's head.

"That's better, isn't it, darling?" whispered Amanita.

Chanterelle did not think so. Once again, the hunger pangs began to bite. She tensed herself against the pain. Amanita seemed to sense that, and to guess its source.

"Poor thing," she murmured. "There's nourishment aplenty at the house, but we must soothe the distress before then, must we not?"

Both her hands were occupied in supporting Chanterelle's body, but the fay leaned forward over her burden, and touched Chanterelle's forehead with her own, very tenderly.

Immediately, Chanterelle felt the sensation of hunger begin to ease, and a welcome torpor spread through her head. And suddenly, she did feel capable of sleep…but was dimly aware that it was, somehow, the wrong kind of sleep. She had wanted to sleep in order to dream, to enter into a kind of trance in which she was still conscious, capable of memory, and an illusion of speech and action, but the sleep that Amanita was inducing in her was an absence, an oblivion.

She tried to fight, but she was not strong enough.

The last thing she heard was Amanita murmuring "It's for the best, my darling. Trust me, it's for the best."

Meanwhile, Catrianne, who was bringing up the rear of the party, was also struck by the impression of Amanita's cape, which seemed paradoxical. In the cabin, it had not reflected the pale light in such a way as to reveal its red color, and the entire cloak had seemed uniformly black. Here, though even though the diffuse light seemed similarly colorless, its bloody hue had become obvious, at least to her eyes.

*I should not be astonished by th*is, Catrianne thought. *If she is, in fact, a fay—and how can I doubt it, in the circumstances?—then she is a magical creature, as the mere fact that we have light to guide us through a pitch-dark forest, whose uncommonly recalcitrant undergrowth politely makes way for us, surely proves. Do I seem somewhat magical myself, not only moving with the same ease through the undergrowth, but gliding along, hardly able to feel my feet touching the ground, simply because I am in her wake, or because there is magic lurking within me that is able to express itself hereabouts because it is finally at home? Would I even be able to follow her if I were not what she claims: part fay myself?*

If what Amanita said was true, Catrianne supposed, then the old crones, unreliable as they were in almost every other matter, had been correct in saying that her mother was a changeling—but not a mere simulacrum put in place of a child the fae-folk wanted to steal, a disguised animal or lump of wood. If some such exchange had been worked, then the baby born to the woodcutter's wife had been exchanged for a fay child, intruded like a cuckoo into the nest of the human community of the forest. But why? What possible reason could fays have for stealing human babies, and even if they had a reason to do that, what further reason could they have for sacrificing babies of their own in exchange.

Did fays even have babies? she wondered. There was little mention of them in the tales that people invented about such creatures. But if Amanita really was a fay, she had a sister, which implied a mother, and a birth. And Melusine, evidently, had a daughter, which similarly implied a birth.

And if Lucinia had been a fay-child, Catrianne realized, and Alastor had been half-fay and half-human, like herself, then Handsel and Chanterelle must be more fay than human...as Chanterelle certainly seemed to be, now that she was in her true environment. Was that what made Handsel so precious, in Amanita's eyes? Fay husbands seemed to be rare in the tales that were told of the fae-folk; although there was occasional mention of them, and even of a fay king, the great majority of tales of fays depicted them as seductive women beguiling human men, for various mysterious reasons, in which amour did not seem to feature frequently, although it was occasionally intense.

For a moment, that caused Catrianne to wonder about Lucinia, and the possible sincerity of her abiding love for Alastor…but that notion was almost immediately displaced by more egotistical concerns.

Is that, she wondered, *the reason why I have never felt the slightest flicker of amour for a man? Is that why the only love of which I seem to be capable is love for my brother and his children? Is it the fay in me that renders my so unhuman in that regard? Is it the fay in me that supplies and guides my talent for music? Am I neither one thing not the other, spoiled as a fay by my human part and spoiled as a human by my fay part, unable to function properly in either world?*

But then she thought about Alastor. If it were still possible for her to entertain the possibility that Lucinia's apparent love for Alastor had been simulated, a trick of seduction, she surely could not think the same about his love for her. That had been utterly honest, and wholehearted. But that did not necessarily mean that it could not have been induced by magic, by fascination. What was amour, after all, but a species of magic, a species of fascination? A species of fascination to which she herself, it seemed, was not vulnerable.…

The questions had become a turmoil in her mind, and the turmoil was becoming an inextricable tangle, like the one that the vegetation was forming behind her, after having moved discreetly sideways, in some strangely sinuous fashion, to give her passage. Amanita, she thought, must have many of the answers, if not all of them, and had promised to give her those she had. But could anything she said be trusted, given that the universal opinion seemed to be that she was evil? Would any answers she provided be anything but a further layer of complexity, entanglement and confusion?

Handsel suddenly stopped in front of her.

"What's the matter?" she asked him, with an edge of panic in her voice.

"We've arrived," he said. His voice was hoarse.

And they had, indeed, arrived. Amanita stepped aside—in an entirely unmagical fashion, having now stepped on to a lawn of soft chamomile—in order to give Handsel and Catrianne a clear view of her abode.

It was not the kind of meager cabin in which they had found her, but nor was it the kind of magical palace featured in so many fanciful tales of Faerie. It was a house that could easily have been built by human hands—and, Catrianne guessed, probably had been. It was made of stone and brick, secured with gray cement and mortar. It had two stories and a slate roof, pitched so as to contain a mansard. It had wooden window frames—Catrianne counted eight on the façade facing her, containing leaded windows—and a climbing rose decorating the porch in front of the main door. It was surrounded by a garden, with neatly-squared flower-beds and lawns, but no garden wall—simply the forest, which extended seamlessly, so far as Catrianne could tell, all around the dwelling.

Catrianne stepped forward on to the carpet of chamomile.

"You had this built for you," Catrianne observed. "Was it the people from the hamlet?"

"The people of the hamlet do a great deal for me, albeit a trifle reluctantly," Amanita told her. "Why else would they deem me a wicked witch? But they're a poor lot, alas. I have to go much further afield to find real craftsmen. Sometimes, I even have to reach beyond the forest to find what I need, for various tasks of construction. It's ironic, is it not, that one should have to go to a town to find wood-workers of real talent...but I was so used to the necessity that it never occurred to me to wonder, even for a second, whether Alastor Ernand might be part fay, all the more so as he was identified to me as the son of the notorious ironmaster. Oh, the forest has a sense of humor, my dear Catrianne. And to think that Melusine stole such a march on me! But come inside, come inside. You must be exceedingly tired, and hungry. This poor thing is fast asleep already in my arms, even though she, too, thinks that I am some kind of demon."

Catrianne looked at Chanterelle, who seemed to be very peacefully asleep. Then she looked at Handsel, who seemed perfectly at ease in the company of the fay.

And after all, Catrianne thought, *what alternative do I have?*

When the fay opened the door of her paradoxical abode, therefore, Catrianne stepped inside without hesitation, simply going with the flow of the dream that had caught her up, like an irresistible tide.

XII

The House

The oblivion into which Chanterelle had been cast while she was clasped and cradled in Amanita's arms did not endure once she was placed in a comfortable bed with soft sheets and a quilt. Once there, her slumber became shallower, and she became capable of dreaming again. Had she been fully lucid she might well have been glad of that, relieved and hopeful, but she was not yet in a state of mind to know that she was dreaming, let alone to be aware of what the fact that she was dreaming might imply.

In her imagination, she found herself alone by night in a vast and draughty church—vaster by far than any church in the town where she had lived, let alone the village whose curé had offered Catrianne the kind of help that his institution was able to offer. Its wooden pews formed a great shadowy maze and Chanterelle was searching that maze for a likely hiding place—but whenever she found one she would hear ominous footsteps coming closer and closer, until they came so close that she could not help but slip away in panic, scurrying like a mouse in search of some deeper and darker hidey-hole.

She never saw her pursuer, but she felt that she ought to know who he was, and what he must be holding in his gnarled and arthritic hand. She knew, though, that no she-wolf could come to her aid in the place where she was, because werewolves cannot set foot on consecrated ground, no matter how noble their purpose might be, nor how diabolical the schemes they might seek to interrupt. She had to get out of the church, therefore, in order to get away from the old man with the iron needles.

But where was the door?

"Don't be afraid, Chanterelle!" the old man called. "The tales are false; I'm not wicked at all. I would never blind a child, or a bird, in order to enable them to sing. In fact, I help them to see, I enable the scales to fall from their eyes. If only you could see, Chanterelle, you wouldn't be afraid any more."

All the while, the hoarse voice was drawing closer, and closer....

It was not until her panic finally provoked her awakening that Chanterelle became lucid again, and freed herself from the nightmare.

At first, she had no idea where she might be. When she opened her eyes, tentatively, she saw walls hung with light velvet drapes, colored sky-blue and green, a casement with leaded panes through which sunlight was streaming, a clean and neatly-plastered ceiling, a chest of drawers, a large trunk, and an armchair positioned beside the bed in which she was lying, next to a small nightstand. There was no fireplace. The bed had linen sheets, and a quilt patterned in black and blood-red…as black and red as Amanita's cape….

Then she remembered where she had been before going to sleep, and deduced where she must be now. The quilt seemed to be the work of an exert seamstress. Amanita? She thought not. The quilt gave the impression of having been sewn with an iron needle, and Chanterelle suspected that Amanita, unlike the deceptive pursuer in her dream, who knew the secret of making nightingales sing by day, might well have an aversion to iron.

Through latticed window, Chanterelle could see treetops, but there was a gap between the window and the forest—between the house and the forest, that is. Although situated deep within the forest, and surrounded by it, Amanita's house was not an intrinsic part of the forest in the way that Melusine's cabin had seemed to be. It was situated in a lacuna.

The door to the bedroom opened discreetly, and her brother stuck his head around it. He gave the impression of having been up and about for some time. As soon as he saw that his sister was awake, he threw the door wide open rushed to her bedside.

"Isn't this wonderful?" he said, gesturing with his arm to indicate the room in which she had been placed. "I have one of my own, and Catrianne's is even bigger. Amanita's must be larger still. Can you imagine?"

"We don't need to imagine," Chanterelle pointed out. "We can see it now, in broad daylight."

Handsel sat down in the chair beside the bed. He was wearing clean clothes: a jacket and trousers in russet brown, a white shirt, brown hose and soft leather shoes, all of which seemed to fit him perfectly. "Don't get up," he said. "You were exhausted, last night. Amanita says that you need rest, and time to recover. How's your ankle?"

Chanterelle was about to reply: "Fine," when she actually tried to move the ankle that she had caught in the hole. It was stiff, and painful. She threw back the quilt and the sheets, and saw that it had been bandaged, She saw, too, that she was wearing a white cotton night-gown much too big for her. She felt quite comfortable, so long as she did not try to move the foot, but she suspected that she might not be able to stand on it without suffering agony. Perhaps the injury was a belated effect of the stumble. Or....

"It's all right," said Handsel, whose voice was no longer hoarse. "You have all the time in the world to let it get better. You must be hungry. I'll bring you some bread—it's freshly baked—and some soup."

"Where's Catrianne?" Chanterelle was quick to ask.

"I'll tell her you're awake."

Handsel left the room—passing through a doorway that had been shaped into a perfect rectangle by a master carpenter, and into which the door fitted very snugly. It opened again almost immediately, and Catrianne slipped in. She too was wearing clean clothes, but they were not as good a fit as Handsel's, presumably having come from Amanita's wardrobe.

"Thank God," said Catrianne, as she sat down in the armchair. "For a while there, I was afraid you might not wake up. I didn't realize that you were so badly hurt...I should have carried you myself. You mustn't worry, though—I don't think we're in any danger. I think it's true, what she says—that I'm half-fay and you're more than half. We're her kin. She has no reason to hurt us...."

Before she could say any more the door opened again, and Amanita came in. "Handsel told me that you were awake," she said. "He'll bring you breakfast in a minute. Did you sleep well, my darling?"

"No," said Chanterelle. "Not well at all."

"That's a shame—but there aren't enough chairs in here. Catrianne, my dear, would you be kind enough to bring a chair from your room, so that Chanterelle can entertain more than one visitor at a time while she's confined to bed?"

Catrianne hesitated momentarily, but then stood up and left the room, allowing Amanita to replace her.

"Your aunt is right," said Amanita. "I have absolutely no reason to wish you harm—but there's a great deal that I need to explain before you'll be able to believe me. When Handsel comes back I'll ask him to fetch another chair, so we can all sit comfortably. But you must eat first. You need to get your strength back, and you must be terribly hungry."

Until Amanita had said that, Chanterelle's hunger had become dull again, and unobtrusive but once she was reminded of it, it immediately flared up again.

Amanita leaned forward. "I know you're afraid, child. Terrible things have been said about me. But you need me, my darling, and you need explanations that only I can give you."

"Or Melusine," said Chanterelle.

"No, child, even she couldn't tell you all that I can tell you, if she's still in a condition to tell you anything at all. There are things she doesn't know, and things she doesn't understand, just as there were things I didn't know and didn't understand, until the forest brought you to me. Our future is at stake, Chanterelle—yours, mine, and the forest's. Perhaps we can't do anything about it, and simply have to let the dream take its own course—but neither Melusine nor I have ever accepted that, or ever will. We'll fight it to the death, and beyond, in our different ways…and I truly am very sorry that differences of opinion have led us to fight one another as well. If only we'd been able to work together…but that's water under the bridge. Here's Handsel. Have something to eat…but take it slowly. You have time to appease your hunger before I tell my story."

Handsel had, indeed come back into the room, carrying a tray that bore a basket of bread rolls, a bowl of hot soup and a cup of milk. Chanterelle sat up, and looked at the contents of the tray suspiciously when it was set down on her lap. Did the bread really have the odor and the color of real white bread, and did the milk have the color and viscosity of real milk, from a cow or a goat? So far as she could tell, yes…but she had a vague suspicion that the appearances were deceptive.

The soup was made with mushrooms and herbs, tinted orange and green.

"The best chanterelles in the realm grow in Broceliande," Amanita told her. "I know that because I'm one of the very few fays who have ever left the forest in order to go to the city. A horrible place, the city… and it ages one terribly. At least I've always had power enough to restore my youth. Melusine…well, the others thought that she'd had other troubles as well, which had inflicted irremediable stigmata, although she always insisted that Lucinia was a pure fay…and now, who could doubt it any longer? But I'm getting ahead of myself. Eat, child, eat."

Chanterelle took a tentative sip of milk. It tasted sweet and creamy. She dipped a piece of bread in it and nibbled the dampened corner. It tasted delicious. But still, she was suspicious of it, and even more so of the soup. But she was very hungry, and she knew that whatever else Amanita might be lying about, she certainly wasn't lying about the fact that Chanterelle needed to eat in order to recover her strength.

"Please believe, Chanterelle," said Amanita, softly, "that the last thing in the world I'd want to do is poison you. "The herbs will help your recovery and make you feel better. I have no way of knowing, but I doubt that Melusine fed your father on anything significantly different, and that, believe me, is not what bound him to your mother, if any binding needed to be done, other than natural human lust."

In the end, Chanterelle decided that if she was prepared to eat the bread and milk, there was little point in avoiding the soup. She ate, patiently and moderately. Her hunger pangs eased, and she really did begin to feel a great deal better.

In the meantime, Amanita sent Handsel to fetch a third chair, and they all sat down in a curved row alongside the bed. Amanita retained the place beside Chanterelle's pillow, next to the nightstand, while Catrianne had sat down next to her, and Handsel had taken the position nearest to the foot of the bed.

"That's good," said Amanita, seemingly satisfied with Chanterelle's obedience. "Now, I can begin. I know that you're all eager to hear what I have to say, and I apologize if some of it is a little too abstruse for a child's mind…but you, at least, Catrianne, ought to understand most of it.

"I can't expect you to believe what I say automatically, I suppose, not just because you've been led to think that I might try to deceive you, but also because it's hardly believable, and I can't entirely guarantee its accuracy myself—but everything I'm about to tell you really is what I believe to be true, and it includes the reasoning behind my own motives and projects. I ought to admit right away that I have done things that humans consider to be evil, and which you might still consider to be evil, even though you now know that you're only partially human—but I had my reasons, and I'm not ashamed of what I've done. I won't hide what I've done from you, because I'd like you to understand, if you can."

She paused, as if waiting for a reaction, but all three of her listeners were waiting, in expectation.

"Good. I really don't know where the story ought to begin, so I'll begin with myself, and Melusine, and try to fill in the background as I go. Melusine and I are twins, although we're far from identical, as human twins sometimes are. It's very rare for fays to have children at all, whether they're in human or any other form, and twins…well, I certainly don't know of any other examples, and there are none even in the tales we tell.

"Some of the tales of the fae-folk that humans tell one another really did originate with the fae-folk, although many are purely products of the human imagination, and most of those that crossed over were distorted in the process. Naturally, those that have crossed over, carrying a little distorted wisdom with them, deal with interactions between fae-folk and humans, usually involving fae-folk who have adopted human form, voluntarily or otherwise. Melusine and I were born with human form, and have retained it throughout our lives—which is also unusual, although by no means unprecedented.

"I ought to explain, because it's crucial to the whole story, that fae-folk come in many forms, and often change form….or did, in the days before the forest began to die. What might be thought of as our original or most primitive form would probably be described by humans—and, indeed, sometimes is, in their tales—as phantasmal, or nebulous, and when fays take on more evident substance or shape, it always used to conserve a certain mutability, although that mutability seems to have been compromised in recent years.

"You might know one of the stories that made the crossover from our lore to yours, concerning a fay who lived a long time ago, named Melusine, like my sister, who married a human, but was obliged to instruct him not to try to see her at certain times, when her shape shifted uncontrollably. He disobeyed the prohibition and saw her in the process of metamorphosis, which horrified and disgusted him. I'm not sure what moral human tellers of the tale attach to it, but among my kind, it was told as a warning against the essential treachery of human beings, and their incapacity to control their impulses, especially their curiosity.

"It was a bad decision on my mother's part to name one of her daughters Melusine, because the legendary association of that name with a fay unwise enough to have intercourse with a human assisted suspicions cast on her when she and I began interacting with humans—suspicions that were inevitably intensified when she gave birth. I confess that I, too, was never completely convinced, until now, that Lucinia was pure fay, although I knew Melusine far better than anyone else, and had every reason to trust her assurances. The pronounced appearances of aging that she took on, however, seemed clear proof that she really had had intercourse with human males, and how, given that, was it possible for anyone, even me, to accept her assurance that the intercourse in question had had nothing to do with her conception?

"I went abroad among humans myself, for exactly the same reasons as Melusine, but I was…more careful, I suppose, or more contemptuous. I was at any rate, more successful at keeping men at a distance: their amorous impulses, if not their insatiable curiosity. I never had the slightest desire to be intimate with any of them. But we thought it necessary to venture into their midst, and not merely on the forest edge, or even villages and towns. We were obliged to go all the way to the capital city in the plain.

"Perhaps that boldness—recklessness, some called it—was responsible for the fact that we became so firmly stuck in human form, but I doubt that it was simply a punishment. It was in any case, necessary. The forest was dying. We were dying. It was no longer adequate simply to live and let the dream take its course, because the dream had already betrayed us, had already abandoned us. When the forest was healthy, it could be reckoned a kind of paradise for all its inhabitants, even though the lives of animals and humans are short and frequently painful, where-as ours—the life of all of the fae-folk—was long and relatively pain-free. There was a harmony about the whole, and a capacity for endurance, but that had been lost long before our anomalous birth. Melusine and I were born into a world in rapid decay, a world whose end was foreseeable in our lifetimes, albeit not in that of the brute humans with whose basic appearance we seemed to have been permanently cursed.

"The incentive to attempt to do something about the prospect of our imminent extinction was powerful, for all the thinking fae-folk, and most powerful of all for those cursed—or gifted—with human brains along with human hands and breasts, whether temporarily or permanently. We had to make an attempt to do something about the fact that our world—or our fraction of the world—was dying. And the ones on whom that responsibility was incumbent, perhaps paradoxically and certainly ironi-cally, were the fays equipped with stable simulacra of human brains, and therefore capable of studying human lore, and trying to discover whether the knowledge that was so effective in transforming their fraction of the world might also be capable of saving ours.

"It wasn't just a whim on the part of Melusine and myself, therefore, to leave the forest for the city with a view to studying human civilization and its legacy of knowledge. It was a mission on behalf of our kind, and all the fae-folk: a mission that all those capable of thinking endorsed and approved. And it was, therefore, monumentally unjust of them sub-sequently to consider us tainted because of it—not just Melusine, who was suspected of intimate human intercourse, but me too, in spite of the careful maintenance of my virginity and my appearance.

"The covert suspicion and animosity generated among our own kind was subdued, however, by comparison with the suspicion and animosity we generated among humankind, even while they had no good reason for thinking that we were anything other than the humans we appeared to be. Melusine's closer intercourse didn't save her from stigmatization with the name of witch or the implications that went with it, even when no formal accusations of spell-casting were made and we weren't de-nounced to those who tortured, hanged and burned some of the poor humans thus stigmatized—the only humans, I will readily admit to you, for whom I ever felt an atom of sympathy.

"I have always retained the attitude with which I first went into the human world: that humans constitute a dangerous alien species, who were, if not the conscious instigators, at least the uncaring instruments of the murder of Broceliande, and were thus our deadly enemies. They were ripe for exploitation, by virtue of their amorous impulses if not their passionate curiosity, and I set out to exploit them, ruthlessly. If they called me witch, I accepted the label, and used the power of the term to make them fear me, and make them serve me. I killed them, when it was convenient, or injured them in other ways. Why should I not? Were they not killing my entire world, destroying the fabric of the mind that had created all the wonderful, fragile fae-folk? Believe me, I would have massacred them all if I could, and danced on their collective grave, and the same is true of the great majority of thinking fae-folk, including, and especially, those who were enabled to think by means of simulacra of human brains.

"Melusine, as you have probably guessed, was one of those who thought differently, but I'll come to that in time. For the moment, the point I need to make is that my powers as a so-called witch were significantly overestimated by the human imagination. I cannot cast spells, read minds or foretell the future by other than the rational or intuitive means that humans have. Yes, there is magic about me, even when I am in the city, let alone at home in the forest, and some of it is an effect of my conscious will—but far less than I could wish.

"Even the magic that really is a matter of action on my part is more akin to the digestion of food, the beating of my heart, or the dilation of my pupils in response to changes in the intensity of light rather than the result of conscious efforts of will. Perhaps consciousness can be trained to a certain influence over fae magic, just as it can be trained to exercise a certain influence over the operation of the gut, the heart and the eye, but it is difficult in the extreme.

"By virtue of that fact, magicienne as I am, I can only kill by the means that the humans whose appearance has been foisted upon me can kill….which is, as you will understand, a very moderate capacity for massacre. Destroying humankind violently was never a practical option for the thinking fays, although its lack of practicality did not prevent some of us from nursing the ambition and attempting to plan projects for achieving it, slowly and subtly, since it manifestly could not be done swiftly and directly.

"Witches are routinely accused by humans of causing plagues and disasters, and doubtless the poor humans caught up in waves of insane persecution wish that they really could do that, as desperately as fays in human form, but they cannot—and nor can we, alas. Perhaps there is a process of education or a trick that might enable such powers, but if so, we were not able to find it…and, as you know from bitter experience, fays separated from the living forest are as vulnerable to plagues and disasters as humans are."

Again, Amanita paused to scan the faces of her listeners. Catrianne nodded to signify that she was keeping up with the argument thus far, albeit with difficulty. Handsel did not manifest any reaction. Chanterelle met Amanita's interrogative glance with one of her own, as if she were questioning everything that she had been told. She had finished the soup, and had almost finished the milk, but she was still nibbling the last morsel of bread.

Amanita sighed, although it was not immediately obvious to her listeners what the sigh signified. Then she resumed her story.

"It is now far too late, I believe, to attempt any kind of wholesale destruction of humankind. No such plan can possibly work. I dare say that you are glad about that, and you are surely entitled to be, being part-human, but I hope you an understand that I cannot share your pleasure, even though I have accepted, resignedly, the inevitability of the death of Broceliande: the death of my true parent—my creator—and the triumph of its murderers, whose form I am cursed to wear, as a kind of final insult.

"Once, however, my predecessors did make plans for countering the human tide, and sought ways of researching such methods. Even recently, as you also know from experience, some of my cousins still thought that there might be information to be gleaned by stealing human children for study and placing simulacra in their cribs, who might grow up not realizing that they were not human until the revelation could be made to them, when they were of an age to become agents capable of spreading seeds of destruction.

"You already know something about the dismal failure of that stratagem, which was always ludicrous. The changelings were often detected and stigmatized; the stolen humans could not adapt to life in the heart of the forest, and almost invariably perished. The changelings often died prematurely too, and it was very rare for them to live long enough to give birth to children, as your mother contrived to do, Catrianne. Even had those problems not emerged, however, there was one crucial limitation of the changelings that would always have limited their effect as agents in the human world: they were all female.

"I confess that I have no idea why that should be the case. It makes no sense to me. If Broceliande can make simulacra of human beings and animals so easily, why can it not make simulacra of males as easily as simulacra of females? That fays in their original form should not be differentiated by sex is natural enough, but given that absence of differentiation, why do they automatically become female when they undergo metamorphosis into more lumpen material form? Humans clearly have no idea, as the tales they make up about the fae-folk, or modify from those they borrow, sometimes take it for granted that there must be fay husbands of one kind or another. The fact is, however, that there are no male fays.

"There are, however, as you know very well, occasional male children born to fays who have had intercourse with humans. There are male demi-fays, and it now seems—in at least one example, although perhaps only one—that male children can be born to a fay who has intercourse with a male demi-fay."

"You mean me," supplied Handsel.

"Indeed," said Amanita. "And we might therefore assume, or at least speculate, that if you were to have intercourse with a fay, you might enable her to give birth to a male child who is very nearly pure fay…a marvel. At least, that might have been practicable once, when Broceliande was not as close to death as it is now, and we were far more numerous than we are, although it would certainly be difficult now.

"I ought not to forget, though, that my information is necessarily limited. Broceliande was once vast, encompassing many mountains ranges, and I cannot be entirely certain that this enclave is the only one in which some life still subsists. More speculatively, one of the things that Melusine and I learned in the course of our investigations is the true size of the world. Our ancestors used to take it for granted that Broceliande was the whole of it, and entirely alone, but I have learned geography enough to know that there are other continents, other forests, and perhaps…only perhaps…there have been, or are, other entities like Broceliande.

"But that is by the by. We—by which I mean the four of us, Melusine, and perhaps a handful of other fays and a few dozen demifays scattered throughout the neighboring region—can only concern ourselves with Broceliande, or the fragment of its former extent that still sustains us…."

"Just a second," Catrianne put in. "*Perhaps* a handful of other fays? Don't you know how many you are?"

"Of course not," Amanita replied. "I had no idea that the three of you existed yesterday, although I admit to being foolish in not having glimpsed some such possibility. My reputation has spread, even in the human world, but that might be the very reason why other surviving fays, in human form or otherwise, might refrain from revealing themselves to me. I am isolated now, but that might be as much the result of ostracism as the annihilation of my peers. In a way, I hope that it is, in much the same say that I truly hope that Melusine is alive and well, even though she disappeared at the same time as Lucinia, and has proved just as difficult to find. I truly hope that she is acquainted with others of her kind, whether in human or other form, and is on good terms with them. I would not wish to harm any of them, and would be glad to greet them as fellows, even if they had ideas similar to Melusine's rather than mine. I have not the slightest conscience regarding the murder of humans, but I have the utmost respect for my own kind, whatever Melusine might have feared."

Chanterelle suddenly interrupted. "What did you do to my grandfather?" she asked, point-blank.

For the first time, Amanita seemed hesitant. Then her shoulders sketched an imperceptible shrug. "I was getting to that," she said. "I wasn't going to hide it—but there are one or two things that it would have been convenient to explain first. I didn't kill him, but although fays only have the same ways of killing as humans have, they do have other… influences. He contributed to his own distress in no small measure, but I'm prepared to take the responsibility, if you wish. I helped him to go mad, and thus bring about his own destruction. I didn't kill him directly, but he is dead, and I'm partly culpable. He died in the forest."

"Why did you do it?" Chanterelle asked.

"Because he was an iron-master, my darling. I did it in order to close the foundry, at least for a while. Doubtless someone else will take it over…and if I can contrive an opportunity to drive them mad or poison them, I'll take it. Like humans themselves, iron is merely an instrument of the forest's death; it has no malice—but still, it *is* an instrument. Assisting the iron-master to die was a petty gesture, I know, but time is short now, and may be of the essence. Perhaps, if I had known that he had married a fay and had children by her…but no, that was a long time ago. If I had known you, and you had pleaded for his life…well, yes, I would have granted you that….perhaps even the foundry…but it's done now. If you feel obliged to hate me for that, so be it…but hear me out, please, and allow my other actions and arguments to carry their own weight…."

XIII

The Story of the Kithara

Chanterelle had nothing else to say, for the moment, and nor had Chatrianne.

Perhaps I ought to be horrified, the latter thought. *Perhaps I am, indeed, obliged to hate her, for having contributed to my father's death… but can I? I was obliged to love him, as my father, and I did, although he never showed any real sign of loving me. Perhaps he was as incapable of that as I am of loving men, and I owe that as much to his blood as my fay mother. The simple truth is, though, that I do not care that Amanita hated my father and plotted his death. It was inconvenient to find the foundry empty when I was forced to return to it for help, but after all, Chanterelle was surely right: this is where we belong, this is the help that we need, far more than any that is available from the village church, or might have been available at the foundry had my father not abandoned it.*

In the meantime, Amanita continued her explanation.

"Where was I? Oh yes…concerning ourselves with Broceliande, and the possible preservation of this fragment of its life and its dream…or, alternatively, the preparation for some kind of regeneration or rebirth, in the near or far future. Both possibilities appeared worthy of investigation and contemplation by Melusine and myself when we undertook our research, although only the former involved any corollary possibility of our own personal longevity. If a fraction of the life and dream of Broceliande can somehow be preserved and protected, then we and a small number of other fae-folk might be able to survive within it; but if the only viable option is to let the dream die with the mind of the forest, while preparing a seed for some potential rebirth in a distant future, our personal survival would be out of the question.

"That became the seed of the difference between my sister and myself—perhaps inevitably, given that she was already aging visibly, and tacitly condemned to death, whereas I was able to maintain the apparent youth of my form, and had the manifest potential of a much longer life. Not that either of us ruled either alternative out of consideration, of course, but we did develop different priorities, and hence the potential for future conflict. Before making any plan, however, we had to cultivate a far better understanding than we had inherited regarding the nature of Broceliande, and the possibilities that might exist of exercising an influence upon it. That, as you can doubtless imagine, was challenging.

"You might think that the human lore we studied in the hope of learning more about Broleliande would have been utterly useless, as humans had no idea that Broceliande existed, and that the great forest that it had already hacked to pieces had a mind that, although not capable of conscious thought, was capable of actions of creations of which no human mind was capable. Those actions and creations had long been described by our own folk-wisdom by means of terminology that can be most readily translated into your language as the forest's dream, and we had grown used to characterizing ourselves as the figments of that dream.

"That is an artificial analogy, for there is no word in our language or yours that can accurately describe the nature of the forest's mentality, for the simply reason that it is beyond their imaginative scope, but the analogy is by no means inappropriate. There are some significant analogies between the dreams of humans and fays and the forest's creativity. There are, however, other affinities between human and fay mentality and the mentality of the forest, and one of them is to do with their relationship with music, and in particular with birdsong and human song.

"Our studies informed us soon enough that the relationship between the human mind and music is as mysterious as the relationship between the fay mind and music, and the relationship between Broceliande and music. There was no explanation of that to be found in human so-called wisdom. On the other hand, there was a great deal to be learned from human learning concerning the mathematics of music, means of annotating and orchestrating music, and means of extending the possibilities of playing and designing music with the aid of new instruments. The instruments of elfin music had previously been elementary: simple pipes and drums. We had no stringed instruments or brass instruments. Although the latter were of no interest to us, stringed instruments were interesting, in terms of the possibility of establishing some kind of communicative link with the mind of the forest, and perhaps some way of influencing its dream.

"Melusine and I set about acquiring existing stringed instruments, learning to play them, to adapt elfin music to them, and eventually, to begin to compose new music. That was my primary specialty: the composition of music that might be able to influence the forest's dream, in terms of its creativity and the guidance of the metamorphoses induced in its creations. Initially, I played the instruments myself and sang to accompany them myself, although it became clear to me fairly rapidly that my talents, especially in the latter respect, were limited. There were expert players and expert singers—both human and avian—that seemed to be capable of greater effects. I believed that the best hope of preserving a considerable area of the forest lay in training birds to sing songs that they could pass on to their offspring as mating calls, and to train human singers who could be recruited from, or at least lodged in, the nearby hamlet.

"Melusine, meanwhile, was thinking along narrower lines. Although she had not given up entirely on the possibility of preserving a substantial section of Broceliande's body and its associated mentality, she was increasingly devoting her time and effort to what she called her secret place: a tiny enclave that could not constitute a living space for individual fae-folk, of whatever form, but might, in principle, constitute a kind of seed, a figurative nutshell containing a kernel of Broceliande's mentality, capable of lying dormant for hundreds, thousands, or even millions of years…until human beings had destroyed themselves."

"Destroyed themselves?" Catrianne queried. "They show no sign of doing that, even with the aid of the new weapons they invent all the time."

"*They?*" queried Amanita, in a satisfied tone. "Are humans already *they* to you, then, my dear demifay?"

Catrianne blushed. "It's a manner of speaking," she said.

"And of feeling," said Amanita. "What about you, Handsel? Do you still think of humans as *us*, as you did yesterday?"

"I don't know," said Handsel cautiously. Catrianne noticed that his hand was unthinkingly palpating the pouch in which he had stowed the pipe he had picked up in the forest.

"Chanterelle?" said Amanita, looking at the little girl with a confident half-smile.

"To be a fay, or a demifay," said Chanterelle, "doesn't necessarily mean hating everything that isn't. Melusine, it seems, didn't hate humans. Humans are perfectly capable of loving other species as well as one another."

"Do you think so?" asked Amanita. "I'm inclined to doubt it, for all their protests. They have a religion that bids them love one another, but which leads the way in torturing and murdering those suspected of the purely imaginary crime of heresy. That speaks to a sense of irony, or self-delusion, but does not bode well for the potential of the species to avoid self-destruction, let alone the possibility that any of the species they claim to love will avoid destruction at their hands."

"There are men like Zebedee," was all that Chanterelle said in opposition to that.

"Zebedee? Ah yes…I know the name. Your father's master and tutor, was he not? Well, I'll take your word for it that he was good, and that there are others like him…but not that they are anything but lambs who will go to the slaughter, when human passions have free rein, and their means of mass destruction have become sufficiently powerful. But let's not digress too far. I still have things to tell you that you need to hear."

She glanced at Catrianne, as if asking for permission to continue. Catrianne nodded.

"Whatever the future might hold," Amanita went on, "Melusine, and those thinking along the same lines, thought it possible, at least, and perhaps inevitable, that there would come a day when something akin to Broceliande would be engendered once again, and might be capable of receiving some legacy from its predecessor. To that end, Melusine's predecessors began making a record of fay lore, including our history and our music—in our own language, of course, not the one we had learned in order to live and study among humans, and which we used for our more abstract discussions, especially of music, for which our native tongue lacked the necessary vocabulary. Melusine eventually inherited that project.

"Melusine believes—and I agree with her—that music might be a means of inducing the dying forest to produce the requisite kernel, the crucial imperishable figment of its expiring dream that might permit the germination of that dream in some far-flung future, when the world could become a harmonious forest once again, devoid of humans—or, at least, the kind of humans who thought in terms of domesticating fire and iron, of building cities and filling the landscape with crop-fields and pasturelands, only retaining paltry stands of trees devoid of any mentality and incapable of creation.

"That became the focus of her ambition and her obsession long ago, but was apparently never the whole of it. Having accepted—as I was not prepared to accept—that it was impossible to protect and preserve a part of the forest large enough to provide a living space for a population of fae-folk and a few carefully-domesticated humans, she apparently took up the threads a second plan conceived by our predecessors for having something of us to survive.

"There have always been demifays, of course, for as long as humans and fays in human form have been living in proximity, but they were always rare, and always likely to become outcasts from both societies, not necessarily regarded as abominations, but always looked at somewhat askance, as anomalies, even by those unaware of their nature. It was rare for them to produce offspring even with humans, and such offspring as they did produce similarly tended to sterility. When our kind became painfully aware of the impending death of Broceliande, however, some of us began taking more interest in demifays, primarily as possibly agents in the quest of sowing death and destruction among humankind, and making some contribution to the ultimate destruction of the species, but also as a kind of reservoir maintaining a vestige, or a phantom, of fay identity.

"The former possibility was of some interest to me, I admit, but the latter seemed to me to be an illusion. Not so to Melusine, though, although I had not suspected, until yesterday, the action she had taken action in that regard. I had always suspected, as I said, that Lucinia was a demifay, in spite of Melusine's denials, and that her interest in demifays was a simple corollary of that fact rather than an aspect of a project. Her interest was understandable, given that she had a daughter, of whatever sort, and hence a conduit to posterity.

"I was intensely interested in Lucinia myself, not for that reason, which seemed irrelevant to me, but because she had such a remarkable singing voice, far better than my own, or those of any of the human singers I kept and trained in the hamlet—my nightingales, as I call them, partly because I routinely conduct their choral training by night. Lucinia, even more so than her similarly-talented but more mature mother, had a truly melodious, crystalline, uncorroded voice.

"It was for Lucinia that I designed the kithara, based on an ancient Greek model but incorporating all the wisdom I had been able to accumulate during my various phases of study in the city, over a period of several decades. Originally, I entrusted its manufacture to the best craftsman in the hamlet, but he proved woefully inadequate to the task. I made enquiries, and soon heard from more than one source that the finest instrument-maker in the entire region was Alastor Ernand, the son of an iron-master and the pupil of the once-renowned Zebedee. Wary of approaching him myself, I employed a go-between to transmit the commission.

"Alastor delivered the instrument a few days late, but I did not attribute any significance to that fact, being glad to receive it at all. I soon ascertained that it lived up to all my expectations. I had already told Melusine of its impending arrival, my plans for its usage, and the role that Lucinia was to play in those plans. We quarreled about that; Melusine was perfectly happy to allow Lucinia to accompany the instrument, but she wanted to confine its use to her secret place, in pursuit of her own scheme. I refused, insisting that, if I were to allow the instrument to be used in that way at all, then Lucinia must also lend herself to my plans, and devote herself wholeheartedly, in the long term, to the continuing attempt to maintain a much larger enclave of Broceliande.

"I suppose that I might have given Melusine the impression, or caused the anxiety, that I might attempt to subject Lucinia to the same kind of fascination and temporary mental enslavement that I employ on my nightingales, but I doubt that that was the reason she decided to send her away. I believe, now, that she always had a plan of her own regarding Lucinia's future, and seized an opportunity to put it into action when it was unexpectedly presented to her.

"By the time I had tested the instrument delivered by Alastor Ernand, and went to find Lucinia in order to invite her to sing to its accompaniment, she was no longer at the cabin, and Melusine had also gone. Naturally, I assumed that they had gone together. I immediately repented of my anger, and the bitter tone of our recent arguments, and searched for Melusine in order to apologize and patch things up, but I have not seen her since the kithara was delivered. It is possible, I suppose, that she has undergone a metamorphosis, at her own instigation or the whim of the forest's mind, but I am reluctant to believe that. I have always suspected that she was simply hiding from me, somewhere, and that she would have to come back to the forest eventually—and that is why I go back to the cabin regularly, in search of evidence that she or Lucinia has been there.

"It was always my conviction that, wherever Lucinia had gone, she too would come back one day, although that did not prevent me searching for her as best I could. I always knew, obviously, that there had to be a connection between Alastor Ernand's delivery of the kithara and Lucinia's disappearance, but had always taken it for granted that it simply consisted of the one having precipitated the other…I never imagined that Alastor might actually have taken Lucinia with him. I was a fool, blinkered my own ideas. And the idea that Lucinia might marry an iron-master's son, or that an iron-master's son might be a demi-fay….well, such possibilities seemed beyond the limits of plausibility…until last night. Last night, everything changed…and now, everything has to be rethought, and replanned."

Finally, she stopped, having apparently said everything she wanted to say, for the time being.

It was a lot to take in, and there were numerous questions whirling in Catrianne's mind. It was difficult to decide which one to ask first, but she grasped one that seemed likely to provoke a comprehensible answer.

"What was in the letter?"

It was evidently not the first question that Amanita had been expecting; it took her two seconds to realize that Catrianne must mean the letter she had recently sent to Alastor, which had arrived too late to find him alive.

"I never stopped working on the problem," Amanita said. I needed an instrument that I could play myself, more versatile than the kithara. I designed one—a kind of harpsichord, played with the aid of keys and equipped with a large array of strings. Naturally, I wanted the best craftsman available to build it. Now...well, I'll have to do without...but perhaps I won't need it, since I have you."

"Me?" said Catrianne, although her tone indicated that she knew what the fay meant.

"Yes. You have played the kithara, after all, and I have no doubt that you play other instruments as well. Have you accompanied Lucinia's singing often?"

"Yes," admitted Catrianne. "But never again, alas."

"And Chanterelle?"

That question threw Catrianne into a quandary. Amanita had asked Chanterelle whether she sang, and Chanterelle had said no. Catrianne did not want to contradict her.

While she was hesitating, Chanterelle intervened. "Do you know the secret of making nightingales sing by day?" she asked Amanita.

Again, Amanita seemed startled by the question. "I know the story," she said, after a slight paused, "but I also know that it's a myth. The method doesn't work. Not that I've tried it personally, you understand, but in the city, I've seen birds blinded with hot needles by fools who took the story seriously. They do not sing, believe me, by day or by night."

"You don't blind your nightingales in any sense, then?" asked Chanterelle, with the air of a fencer striking a clever blow.

Amanita thought for a full five seconds before answering: "Not literally. I wouldn't do that, even to a human. I certainly wouldn't do it to a bird. But if I take your intended meaning correctly...yes, as I said a few minutes ago, I do exercise a degree of fascination and stern control over the singers I recruit from the villages. But I don't use knives, even on the boys, in the way your churchmen are sometimes said to do. Perhaps I'm wicked...but I'm not a monster. Perhaps I do, in a way, steal children, partially and temporarily...but I don't castrate them, and I release them completely when age deepens their voices."

Chanterelle seemed content with that, but Amanita was quick to riposte. "Will you answer me a question in return for that admission, my darling?"

"What is it?" asked Chanterelle, noncommittally.

"Did your mother tell you the story of how she and your father met?"

Chanterelle barely hesitated before saying: "Yes."

"And that's how you found your way to the cabin last night?"

"Yes."

"And did your father visit Melusine's secret place."

Chanterelle said nothing.

"Yes he did," Amanita deduced—but her expression was pensive rather than triumphant. "With the kithara—and Lucinia?"

Silence was evidently pointless. Chanterelle said: "So mother said."

Amanita frowned. "That's puzzling," she murmured. "That's…but I suppose that's more than one question, my darling," she went on, abruptly changing tack. "You can have another turn, if you have any more."

"What do you intend to do with us?"

That made Amanita laugh. "I intend to offer you hospitality, of course. You're all very welcome to stay in my house for as long as you wish, and I certainly hope that you won't want to leave soon, or ever, but you're not prisoners. You're free to go wherever you want, whenever you wish. I'm not asking for anything in return, although I would certainly be delighted to hear Catrianne play the kithara…and to hear you sing, Chanterelle, if you've a mind to, although I leave that entirely to you. But there is one small favor I'd like to ask all of you, if I may?"

"What is it?" said Catrianne, feeling that she, not Chanterelle, ought to be bearing the burden of the conversation.

"If Melusine makes contact with one of you, please tell her that I really would like to speak with her, as a sister, and to repair the rift between us."

"How will she know that we're here?" Catrianne asked.

"She'll know," said Amanita, confidently. "If she's still alive, she'll know. And if she's dead…but I don't want to believe that…not yet. I wish her no harm, as you know. She doesn't trust me, and never has, but there really is to reason for our past differences to keep us apart—not now. Quite the contrary; there's every reason for us to work together. *Every* reason. Tell her I'm willing."

"Willing to do what?" Catrianne asked.

"She'll understand."

"You said that you were going to explain everything," Catrianne told her, a trifle resentfully.

"I've explained my side of the matter," said Amanita. "It's up to her to explain hers, if she's prepared to do so, and if she can. I'm simply trying to guess what she might have in mind, and I might be wrong. But I'll leave the three of you to talk between yourselves, now that you know what this is all about. It must have come as a terrible surprise to you, given that my dear niece didn't even bother to explain to any of you—except perhaps to Chanterelle—that you're not human."

So saying, Amanita picked up the tray contained Chanterelle's empty plate, glass and bowl from the night-table, and left.

Catrianne was the first to break the silence. "*Did* you know?" she asked Chanterelle.

"Not really," said Chanterelle. "Mother told me the secret stories, but I only had the vaguest notion, until last night, what they might mean. Even now, I don't really *know*. I'm not clever enough, and I haven't dreamed enough."

"Why didn't she tell me?" Handsel complained.

"Because you're only twelve," Catrianne supplied. "When the time came, she would have told us all. Amanita's right. Eventually, Lucinia would have come back here, with Alastor, and with you. The plague spoiled everything. She would probably have told us then, if the fever had given her a chance, but when Alastor died…she just wasn't strong enough."

"Well," said Handsel, "we haven't found a grandmother we never knew anyway, but at least we've found somewhere to live, and not some dingy cabin. It seems to me that we're a great deal better off this morning than we were yesterday."

"That's true," admitted Catrianne. "What if she is a witch? So are we, in the reckoning of all the old crones, and even the curé who wanted to help us. She has no reason at all to wish us harm. Unless you know something we don't, Chanterelle?"

"I don't know anything, yet," Chanterelle insisted, "but I think I might be able to work it out, with a little help…but do you really not care, Handsel, that she drove our grandfather mad? But for that, we might have found shelter at the Foundry."

"Or we might not," countered Handsel. "We weren't sure, remember, that he wouldn't turn us away."

"He wouldn't have," Catrianne was quick to say. "He was my father—and Chanterelle's right; we shouldn't forget that she harmed him, and has no conscience at all about hurting people. That's because she doesn't think of herself as human…but perhaps, since that's the form and nature she has, she should. As for my father…I loved him, but he was a very, very difficult man, and I don't know what would have become of any of us if he had taken us in at the foundry, any more than I know what might become of us here…except that it seems to be a safe haven for the time being, and that the choice is ours of how long we stay, and where we might go if and when we decide that we don't want to stay any longer."

Chanterelle said nothing to that, but her silence was clearly not an assent.

"There's still a lot I don't understand, though," Catrianne was quick to add. "I don't understand why this part of the forest needs saving, let alone how Amanita proposes to save it. Why can't it simply be left to its own devices? It's too high on the mountain for anyone to want to clear it for planning or pastureland, and the timber is far from first rate. I can't imagine that anyone's going to touch it with cold iron for a hundred years."

"It's already dying," said Chanterelle. "Unless it can be helped somehow, it will be dead soon, and the fays with it. They're just extensions of it."

"Will we die too, then?" Handsel asked.

"Possibly," said Chanterelle, "but not necessarily. Even you and I might have enough of the human in us to survive…but only as humans. We'll have lost something. We'll have changed."

"If that's the case," said Catrianne, "surely we ought to help Amanita preserve it."

"If it were as simple as that," said Chanterelle, "Melusine would have wanted the same thing. We need to hear what she has to say—in dreams, if she can't come to us in the flesh. I didn't understand, last night, why something seemed to be trying to stop us reaching the cabin, but it's possible…I can't help wondering whether Amanita might be lying about that."

"About what?"

"That it was just a coincidence that she was in the cabin when we arrived. She was waiting there, but not for us. She was expecting Lucinia. She might have had alarms of some kind planted that told her as soon as anyone stepped off the road. I thought the reason there were obstacles that got in our way was that someone had placed protective devices around the cabin to deter random passers-by, but it's possible that Melusine's agents were trying to deflect us away from Amanita."

"Why?"

"I don't know—but I think Amanita put me into a deep sleep deliberately, so that Melusine…or something…couldn't reach me in a dream. The contest between them isn't over, and we're pieces in the game now. We always were, I suppose. The problem is…."

"What?" prompted Catrianne.

"That even if Amanita really is evil, that doesn't necessarily mean that Melusine is good. Mother certainly thought so…but she would, wouldn't she?"

"That's too convoluted, Chanterelle," Catrianne told her.

"I know," said Chanterelle, with a sigh. "But I'm confused, and my ankle hurts. I need to sleep…to dream."

"Let's wait and see, then shall we, darling?"

"We don't have any alternative, do we?" said Chanterelle, looking at her bandaged ankle, wondering whether she would be able to sleep,

and whether the nagging injury might taint her dreams with nightmare
if she could.

XIV

Lucid Dreams

Once Chanterelle was on her own, after Catrianne and Handsel had gone downstairs to explore the house and its surroundings, promising to report back anything interesting that they saw, she tested her injured ankle by stretching the toes and turning it to the left and the right. She had wondered briefly whether the bandage might be an artifice, to make her think that it was a more serious impediment than it was. The pain she felt, however, and the way it intensified when she moved the foot, proved that she really had hurt herself—or had been hurt. The brief intensification nearly brought tears to her eyes—but the anguish wasn't entirely unwelcome, because it focused her mind, and seemed to stimulate her train of thought.

What I need, she thought, *is to go back to sleep, in order to dream. That's the way to get into touch with the forest, or with Melusine...if I can. But I need to pay careful attention to any dreams I have, if I can. Here in the forest, that's surely possible. My stomach's full now and that should help.*

She lay down, closed her eyes, and tried to stay quite still, in order not to risk twinges of pain from the ankle.

She lost track of time. She had no sensation of drowsiness, but nor did she hear the door to her room open and someone come in. However, when she turned her head slightly to dispel a slight crick in her neck, she saw Amanita sitting in the chair beside her pillow again. She was immediately aware, however, that Amanita hadn't actually come into her room: that what she was seeing was some kind of phantom produced by her own mind.

But that's where the answers are, she thought. *It's just a matter of bringing them out, of discovering what the fragments of the dream really mean.*

"I wish you would eat something, my darling," said Amanita, with a deep sigh. "If you don't eat, you'll never recover your strength."

That seemed to be a poor start: the very opposite of making sense.

"But I have eaten," said Chanterelle. "I ate your bread, your milk and soup, even though I didn't really trust any of them."

Amanita did not seem to hear her. "If you eat," she said, "you might even recover your voice. You mustn't let stories make you afraid—and in any case, you can see readily enough that my house isn't made of gingerbread."

Chanterelle put out a hand to touch the wall beside the bed, feeling the texture of it through the blue-and-green cloth. It was softer than she had expected, and warmer. It had a curious texture unlike any wall she'd ever felt before. It wasn't plaster, brick or stone, and it wasn't wood or wattle-and-daub.

"It's a mushroom," whispered Chanterelle, even though she knew that it was absurd. "The whole house is a gigantic mushroom. How did it grow so big? It must be magic—black magic."

"Magic is neither black nor white, my darling," said Amanita. "Magic just *is*."

"The witch in the house of gingerbread tried to fatten Handsel for the cooking-pot," Chanterelle observed. "She wanted to eat him."

"Did the witch succeed?" asked Amanita.

"No," said Chanterelle. "Gretel put an old stick in the witch's hand every time she reached into the cage to see whether Handsel was plump enough to eat yet. The witch was near-sighted, and couldn't tell that it wasn't Handsel's arm. When the witch grew impatient and tried to cook Gretel instead, Handsel pushed her into her own oven and cooked her. Then the children took the witch's hoard of gold and jewels back to their father, so that they would never be poor again."

"Well," said Amanita, "you can certainly see the human imagination in that. Our kind tell the tale differently. I'm not near-sighted, dear child. Were I a witch, you'd have no chance at all of escaping me, and it wouldn't enrich you in the least to bundle me into my own oven. I have no hoard of gold and jewels, and you have no father. You asked me just now about another story, though, didn't you: the one about a little girl with a marvelous singing voice, who lost the will to sing when her heart was broken, but was found by the old man who knew the secret of making nightingales sing by day. You know how the old man made the nightingales sing by day, even though no one ever told you the end of the story; you know what he did to set free the little girl's captive voice."

"I know," whispered Chanterelle.

"Well," said Amanita, "that's utter nonsense too, as I told you. The secret of teaching the song of the forest isn't by way of blindness, but by way of sight. Hurting you wouldn't set your voice free. All you need is to want to sing, and some good food to nourish you…and then you'd be able to see the forest as it really is, and not as humans see it. You've enough fay in you for that, I'm sure. So has Handsel. Chatrianne hasn't got your advantages, but I'll soon find out whether her musical talent has magic in it, and she seems to be a virgin, so I have high hopes for her too. The forest might not be able to think, but there's method enough in its dream to have brought you here—*to me*. You need to eat more, though. You're as thin as a rake—there isn't enough substance to you to make a bird of any size…and you really wouldn't want to be something as dull and petty as a nightingale. We really need to feed you up."

"You bread isn't really bread, though, and your milk isn't really milk," said Chanterelle. "The bread is baked from mushrooms and the milk is squeezed from mushroom flesh…and not from chanterelles."

"That's true, as it happens," admitted Amanita. "As you've observed yourself, there's not much food fit for children growing wild in this part of the forest. There are insects a-plenty, and a few animals that eat insects, and even fewer animals that eat animals, but children with injured ankles can't go hunting, can they? Fortunately, the mushrooms with the red caps make nourishing food. Handsel is bold and strong as well as handsome, isn't he? He eats plenty of bread and drinks my milk, and he loves the red-capped mushrooms. This afternoon, I'll take him hunting with my greyhounds, and this evening, Catrianne will play the kithara for us, and we'll all be one big happy family, if you'll consent to sing for us. I'll carry you downstairs and you can sit on a perch, and sing. Even to begin with, I'm sure, you'll fill the house with the dream. And that will just be the beginning. We'll sing and we'll sing, and we'll all just be one big happy family for as long as we can sing the dream. One big happy family."

"Ah!" whispered Chanterelle. "I'd rather go home."

"You have no home, remember?" said Amanita. She leaned forward to stare at Chanterelle even more intently than before. "Even the foundry is sold. It had failed long before the plague came and your grandfather tipped the unfinished church bell into the tarn? Do you know why no one can hear it tolling in the dark current, least of all its maker? Because it has no tongue! It cannot chime, dear child—but you can still sing, if you will. I hope that that, with my help, you might even sing the forest alive, if you've a mind to do it. But you need to believe in it…in me."

There was, however, an edge of desperation in her voice. She was the one who needed to believe, and she didn't, yet. Amanita knew that there was something she didn't know, something she had yet to fathom. At least, the phantom Amanita of Chanterelle's waking dream knew that, just as Chanterelle knew it. Neither of them knew, as yet, what this dream-fragment was all about…what's the forest's dream was all about…because even the forest didn't know, and couldn't, because it wasn't yet capable of knowing, of thinking, of planning, of deliberately saving some fragment of itself, now or for the future. It could only rely on the impetus of the dream.

The forest's dream had lasted thousands of years, perhaps far longer, Chanterelle realized, but until recently, even until this very moment, it had never even come close to becoming conscious of its dream.

And now it was almost on the brink of lucidity, it was almost on the brink of annihilation.

The irony of fate.

"Melusine might have other ideas, of course," said Amanita. "But will she consent to tell us what they are? She won't tell me, so why should she tell you? But if she does, my darling, I hope you'll tell me, because I really do need to know. I hold all the cards now, it seems. Handsel is already seduced, although I haven't *quite* made up my mind what to do with him yet, and Catrianne is easy, which brings the kithara fully into play again. I'm going to bring my nightingales here tonight for our little celebration, and our first experiment. Their singing might inspire you to join in. I certainly hope so.

"There really is no point in your being stubborn, Chanterelle. Your mother didn't want to sing for me, and I can see why that might make you hesitate, but she didn't really have any good reason to refuse. She was just doing what her mother told her, like a good girl. But sometimes, parents don't know best. Where would you be now, my darling, if your father had listened to his father, and had meekly become a foundryman, a creature of iron? Where would Catrianne be, if she'd allowed him to marry her off to some metal-dealer? You'd be nowhere, my darling, because you wouldn't exist, and nor would the kithara.

"We have a lot to be thankful for, you and I. We're on the same side, you know, part of the same family…figments of the same dream. Don't try to spoil it, Chanterelle, please—and don't run away from it either. But I must go now, because Handsel and I are going hunting. I do hope that we'll have a successful hunt, because it really would be nice to have some meat for supper, and you really do need to eat, Chanterelle."

"But I have!" Chanterelle protested, as Amanita disappeared.

Chanterelle remained suspended then between consciousness and uncertainty, still not entirely sure whether she was awake or asleep, in spite of the manifest absurdity of some elements of the dream. She could not believe for an instant that Amanita's house really was made of fungus rather than brick and stone, and she was absolutely certain that she had eaten her breakfast, although she was by no means certain that it had been what it had pretended to be.

I need to dream of other things than Amanita, she thought. *I need to dream about Melusine, if I can—although I'm not sure how I'd recognize her if I did. If I can't, I need to see the she-wolf again.*

And, as if on demand, she did catch a glimpse a mournful she-wolf, then, from the corner of her eye, and also a decrepit bear, and two ghostly hunting-dogs that bounded through the forest like malevolent angels.... but she was all too well aware that the dream was becoming chaotic, escaping her grasp.

She tried to focus her mind, but it only seemed to make matters worse, and more nightmarish. Then she dreamed about sweet-smelling loaves of bread that broke to reveal horrid masses of blue-green fungus, of cups of milk infested with tiny worms, of long ranks of club-headed mushrooms that served as cushioned seats for excited fairies, and of wizened old men who knew the secret of making nightingales sing by day.

Relax, she told herself. *Be calm. Let it flow.*

She relaxed, but what seemed to flow, at least for a while, was oblivion. She lost track of herself.

When she found herself again, without any sensation of waking up, the room was nearly dark. The patch of blue sky that had been visible through the latticed window while Amanita was giving her explanation had turned to velvet black, but the stars seemed to be out, and the moon must have been full, for the room was not entirely cloaked in shadows. Even so, it seemed to Chanterelle that oblivion had claimed her for an unreasonably long time, given that the situation was so urgent, not merely from her own tiny point of view but the forest's vast viewpoint.

How terrible it must be, she thought, *finally to reach the brink of wakefulness, after thousands of years of contented dreaming, only to find yourself on the point of death, having been patiently murdered in your sleep, hacked apart by a trillion cuts, with nothing left to live on but the fragments of your dream, which will disappear as all such fragments do unless you can find a way of grasping them, of knitting them together, or somehow making enough sense of them to form a plan...or if not a plan, an idea....or, if not even that, something: a spasm, a gesture, an atom of hope....*

Chanterelle was still trying to figure out what time it was when something caught her attention. At first, she thought it was an insect—a night-flying moth—fluttering into the window repeatedly, as such moths often do: *tap...tap...tap....*

It's a soul, she thought, *the shade of someone dead, trying to attract my attention, but I don't know how....*

Then she realized that the door of the room had creaked, as it began to open. She watched it move inwards, her heart fluttering briefly, because she expected to see Amanita again.

When she saw that the person coming into the room was Handsel, and not Amanita, Chanterelle felt a thrill of relief, which almost turned to joy when she saw the excited expression on his face. For a moment she read that excitement as a sign that he must have found Melusine—but when he came closer she realized that it was something else.

"Oh, Chanterelle!" Handsel whispered, as he knelt down beside the bed and put his head on the pillow beside hers, "You've no idea what a day I've had."

"You've been out hunting with Amanita and her dogs," she remembered. "Are we whispering because you're afraid of waking Amanita?"

"Amanita's not here," Handsel said, in a slightly louder voice. "She must have gone out again with the dogs, to hunt the she-wolf. We chased it all afternoon, but it gave us the slip."

"You hunted the she-wolf?" said Chanterelle, alarmed. "But it's just a figment of a dream?"

"I can believe that. Anyway, we had to give up in the end. Then I ate some more mushrooms—and I gained my sight!"

"You never lost your sight," said Chanterelle, faintly.

"I never had my sight, my dear sister. I always thought that I could see, but now I know that I never saw clearly before today. I had never seen the trees, or the earth, or the air, or the sun. Today, for the first time, I saw the life of the trees, the richness of the earth, the color of the air and the might of the sun. Today, for the first time, I saw the world as it truly is. I saw the fae-folk about their daily business. I saw all the inferior spirits too: dryads drawing water from the depths and breathing for the trees; kobolds churning the soil to make it fertile; sylphs sweeping the sky and undines bubbling the springs. I really am more fay than human, you see, and this is where I belong. Amanita is wonderful!

"Oh Chanterelle, you must eat the mushrooms, as I have, and learn to see as well as to sing! The fae-folk swarm about them, hungry for pleasure, and make them grow tall and red, but there's no poison in them. There's nourishment, for the mind as well as the body. You mustn't be afraid of eating, Chanterelle. You mustn't starve yourself of light and life."

"I don't," said Chanterelle, and shut her eyes for a moment, trying to think. "I'm not."

Tap...tap...tap....

The soul was still there, still trying to get in, stupidly bumping into the window-pane.

Chanterelle knew that the sight that Handsel thought that he'd discovered was the second sight of which certain stories told, which might have crossed over from the tales of the fays, or might simply be the product of the human imagination, but must in either case be related to the dream of Broceliande, to the real dream, to the dying dream. She knew that the second sight, in the tales, was sometimes a blessing and sometimes a curse. She had always thought that if either she or her brother turned out to have the second sight it would be her, and she felt a slight pang of jealousy. She, after all, was the one who could sing—or had been able to sing, before grief had taken the melody out of her voice... perhaps forever.

Tap...tap.......

When she opened her eyes again, Handsel was no longer there—or, if he was, he was no longer Handsel. Kneeling beside her bed was the strangest creature she had ever seen. It was part-human, having human legs and human arms, but it was also part-insect, having the wings and head of a hawk-moth. Where the human and insect flesh met and fused, in the trunk from neck to hip, there was a soft carapace mottled with white stars. Even in the dim light, Chanterelle could see that the color of the carapace was crimson, like Amanita's bloody cape.

The huge compound eyes looked at Chanterelle with what might have been tenderness. The principal part of the creature's mouth was a pipe-like structure coiled like a fern-leaf, which gradually uncoiled and stiffened, so that the tip reached out to caress her face.

When the creature spoke to her, its words sounded as if they were notes produced by some kind of flute, and every sentence was a delicate musical phrase.

But what it said was all wrong. It was as if Handsel—the Handsel produced by her own mind of course, not her actual brother—were still interfering with the moth-soul that was trying to possess him, preventing it from saying what it had come to say by rambling on about the sight he had gained...sight that was momentarily channeled through compound eyes and a tiny, uncomprehending, insectile mind.

"The sweetest nectar of all is the blood of fays," the monster informed her, "but the fae-folk offer it willingly. Human blood is bitter, spoiled as anything is spoiled that is kept for far too long. Iron bells are hard and cold, and their voices are the tyrants of time. The bells of forest flowers are soft and beautiful, and their voices can unloose the bonds of the hours and the days. When humans go mad they usually become bears or wolves, but find neither solace nor liberation. The fae-folk are forever mad, forever joyous, forever free. Children can still be changelings, if they so choose. While the true sight has not quite withered away, children can still find the one true path. While the true voice is not yet lost, children can still soar on wings of song."

If only the monster had chosen its words more carefully, Chanterelle thought, it might have contrived a melody of sorts—but she had heard the songs of the skylarks and thrushes that the city-dwellers kept in cages, and she knew full well that even they had little enough talent for melody. Nightingales, for all their fame, were merely plaintive, and did not sing at all if they were blinded.

Chanterelle shut her eyes again, and counted to ten, hoping that when she opened them again, she might have achieved a degree of clarity.

When she opened them, the monster was, indeed gone, and Handsel seemed to be himself again, at least in the phantom appearance credited to him by her dreaming mind.

"What did you say?" asked Chanterelle, in a voice as faint as faint could be.

"I said that we can be safe and happy here," murmured Handsel, in a whisper that was not quite a lost voice. "Amanita is prepared to adopt us, and if we're good, we be able might live here forever. She'd be lonely without us, wouldn't she? Catrianne's only half a fay, but we're more than that. Amanita can accept us as her own children, if we promise to be good. Wouldn't you like to live in an enchanted forest, Chanterelle?"

"I'd rather be at home," murmured Chanterelle.

"This *is* our home now," said Handsel, "and we ought to be glad of it. What's the alternative? Would you rather starve than eat? Would you rather go down to the valley, where no charity awaits us, than stay in the wild forest and live as the fae-folk have always lived? We have to do what Amanita wants of us, Chanterelle—both of us. She needs us both. Tell her that you will, Chanterelle, please."

"I need to talk to Melusine," whispered Chanterelle.

"I don't think you can," said Handsel said. "I don't believe that Melusine can talk, any longer. In fact, I have this strange feeling that she's dead, and that I saw her die, but didn't realize it, because I'd never recognized her. But even if she isn't dead, I don't believe that she has anything to say. When Amanita comes back with her nightingales, I'll ask her to bring you your supper, and then carry you downstairs. Catrianne's going to play the kithara, and the nightingales are going to sing. You need to be there, even if you won't sing yourself. You need to hear it." He stood up, and turned towards the door.

"Don't go!" said Chanterelle, although her voice was so feeble that she could not make her panic felt.

"I have to," said Handsel. "Be good, Chanterelle."

"But I'm not awake!" Chanterelle protested. "I'm just dreaming."

"No," said Handsel. "That was in the old life, the life of the town, the life that humans are making for themselves, in the service of their own dreams. Now, you're just being dreamt. It's confusing, at first, I know, but you'll get used to it. You have to, because if you don't, the dream will die, and we'll die too. We're part of it now. We have been ever since... well, I was about to say since we stepped off the path opposite the cleft in the rock, but in fact, it's ever since forever. You can't go back, Chanterelle, you can't be what you were, or even what you are. This is where you live, now, and you have to discover what you can be...not what you want to be, because you don't have that choice, but what you can be. I have.

"This is how the fae-folk live, and we're fae-folk now, Chanterelle. Even Catrianne is just one more nightingale, like Amanita's children, but it's just possible that you and I can live forever, if you can only find the right key, the right E. You have to be good, Chanterelle...or better, This is where you exist, now. This is where you have to eat, and drink, and sing. There's no way back."

And so saying, he disappeared. He didn't leave the room; he just disappeared. The door was still open, though, where he had come in.

No sooner was Chanterelle alone than the room grew noticeably darker. A cloud must have drifted across the face of the moon. When someone else slipped into the room and placed herself in the chair beside the pillow, she was no more than a shadow...or a shade.

"Be quiet, Chanterelle," said a familiar voice. "I need to tell you a story...but first I have to collect myself. I've been asleep for a long, long time, but I can wake up, now...."

Chanterelle sat bolt upright. "Mother!" she said "Is that you?"

"No, no, my sister," murmured the shadow. "You don't understand. I'm not who you think I am. I never was. But you must forgive her. She thought it was for the best. It's not her fault. It's what she was...why she was...but I can't tell you here, any more than you can sing here. You need to come to the secret place, Chanterelle—alone. I can tell you the story there, and we can sing together...."

"Shall I bring the kithara?" Chanterelle asked.

"No...there's no need, any longer. Once was sufficient. But listen to Catrianne play, carefully. She doesn't know the music, but you'll get the feel of it, sense the song we need to sing. The forest will provide the accompaniment...at least, I hope so. The story needs an ending, and only the forest can find it, because there's no one else. The rest of us...even you, although you have a little of the human in you...are just figments of the dream, Broceliande's means of trying to see herself, to understand herself...."

"Herself?"

"Of course. She's your real mother, Chanterelle. She's *the* real mother. I'm fading, now, though. Come to the secret place...."

"But I don't know where...," Chanterelle began to say, but interrupted herself. It was true; she didn't know where the secret place was. But she knew, now, that she could find it, and had *almost* guessed what she would find there, and why.

Chanterelle moved her injured foot from left to right and back again, and then she stretched her toes. The result was agony—but it was the kind of agony that chased sleep away, and delirium too.

At last—at long last, it seemed to her—she woke up,

Because she had no voice, Chanterelle cried out silently for her mother, or her sister, begging her to come back, although she knew that the shadow could not return, now.

It's up to me now, she thought. *If I can't figure it out, and quickly, I'll be lost. We'll all be lost.*

But then she was ashamed of herself for giving herself too much importance. What was she, after all, but a little girl...a little girl with a sprained ankle.

She screamed, silently.

In stories, she knew, such silent cries sometimes brought results. In stories, panic was sometimes as powerful as prayer. She prayed as well, though, in the hope that even if her mother couldn't come back, and couldn't help her, Heaven might.

As before, the shock of pain she had induced could not keep sleep at bay for long, but the sleep to which Chanterelle fell back this time was shallow and turbulent.

She dreamed that she was running through the forest yet again, still pursued by the old man who knew how to make nightingales sing by day. All night long his footsteps grew closer and closer, until at last she sank exhausted to the ground and waited for the inevitable.

As before, though, the old man had no chance to complete his dire work. He was knocked flying by the paw of a bear, which then limped away into the forest with its ancient head held low.

When the old man attempted to rise again he was confronted by a she-wolf whose grey coat was flecked with blood. For a moment or two it seemed that the old man might try to defy the she-wolf, which was limping almost as badly as the bear, but when she showed her bright white teeth he thought better of it and ran off, in the opposite direction to the one the bear had taken.

"Thank you," Chanterelle whispered to the she-wolf.

"Don't thank me," said the wolf, sinking down beside her. "I can't help you. I can't even help myself." The wolf began licking at her wounds. Both her hind legs had been bitten, and her belly too. It was obvious that the hounds had almost brought her down.

"Who'll help me if you can't?" asked Chanterelle. "Must I trust in Heaven?"

The she-wolf stopped licking long enough to say: "Heaven is a poor ally to those still on earth, else plague would have no power to consign us to damnation. The world is full of disasters, alas, and ours is only one of them. But Melusine is beyond help already. She can't complain that Heaven didn't save her, in spite of all your prayers. Those who are less than honest can hardly look to Heaven for salvation."

"Then what will become of me?" asked Chanterelle.

The wolf was too busy feeding on its own blood to give her an immediate answer, but when her fur was clean again she looked the child full in the face with sorrowful eyes.

"I wish I knew," the wolf said. "I can't even tell you the answer to your other question."

"What other question?" asked Chanterelle.

"Why the girl sang again when she was captured for a second time by the man who knew the secret of making nightingales sing by day, and was blinded by him, when she could have stayed silent. I don't know the answer. All I know is that there's no more joy in being a wolf than there is in being a bear. I have to go away now. If I stay in this part of the forest the hounds will have me for sure—and a wolf shouldn't have to live on mice while there are sheep in the valleys."

"Please don't go," begged Chanterelle, in a voice so weak as to be almost unheard. "If only you could save me, I think I might be able to sing again."

"Too late," said the wolf. "You have to help yourself now, if you can, and Lucinia too." And she disappeared into the darkness of the forest.

XV

The Awakening

"It's late, my darling," said Amanita, as Chanterelle woke to find the window of her room red with the fires of the sunset, and knew that the night of which she'd just dreamed was still to come. "You must have something to eat now, or it will be too late. Did you sleep well?"

Amanita was sitting no more than an arm's reach away from Chanterelle's head, having sat down in the same chair as before. The white-clad fay was holding a bowl full of steaming soup, which had the most delicious scent. The soup was thick and creamy, with solid pieces of a darker hue half-submerged beneath the surface.

"Mushroom soup," said Chanterelle, very faintly.

"The best mushroom soup in the world," said Amanita. "All mushrooms aren't alike, as you know. These are the very best. I had to hunt far and wide to find them for you, but I knew that I'd have to find them, even if it took all day."

"You were hunting," said Chanterelle. "With Handsel."

"That's true," the fay admitted. "And then I had to go to the village to fetch the nightingales—but all the while, I had my eyes open, and I was carrying a basket to put the mushrooms in. The dogs were chasing a mangy wolf, and the chase took me to parts of the forest I'd never been before. Can you believe that? After the hundreds of years I've lived here. But I suppose I've been away a lot. It was a sacrifice, but needs must. Open your mouth, my darling."

"I don't want it," whispered Chanterelle.

"But you must eat," said Amanita. "You ate this morning, and it didn't do you any harm, did it?"

"No," admitted Chanterelle. "I've been dreaming all day, and I think the soup helped it that…but also increased the confusion. Tonight, I need a clear head, though."

Amanita let the wooden spoon that she had been holding out fall back into the bowl, and dip beneath the surface of the liquid contained there. "Why?" she asked.

"Because I need to listen to the music. I need to concentrate on the song."

"Ah!" said Amanita. "Yes, that's good...or is it? I don't mind admitting, Chanterelle, that I don't understand you at all. I don't know where you figure in the story. Handsel is obvious, Catrianne easily fathomable, but you...you're keeping secrets from me, and I wish you wouldn't. If we're going to live together, as a family, we need to be honest with one another. I can't expect you to love me right away, but I do want you to love me in the end, as I want to love you. We'll have a lot of magic to work, if we're to keep the forest alive and protected."

"I believe you," said Chanterelle, "but I don't think it matters. It's too late. I think the forest feels it too."

Amanita flinched. "You're just a child," she said. "How can you know?"

Chanterelle had no answer to that. She had no idea how she could know. She refrained from riposting: *How can you?*

"I wish you'd eat something," said the fay.

"Tomorrow," said Chanterelle. "I'll eat tomorrow." *If tomorrow ever comes*, she refrained from adding aloud.

As if to underline the unvoiced thought, she heard the distant resonant vibration of a string, as Chatrianne, in one of the rooms downstairs, began to tune the kithara.

"You must," said Amanita. "You need to eat. Will you sing with my nightingales tonight?"

"I can't," Chanterelle told her.

"I think you could if you wanted to," said Amanita, resentfully—but she changed her tone immediately, to say: "but what I really want is for you to want to. I understand that you loved your mother, and took what she told you about me at face value, but I wish you'd give me a fair hearing, now that we're going to live together. We are going to live together, aren't we, my darling? You don't have any alternative, do you?"

"I suppose not," said Chanterelle—and, indeed, there was no alternative that she could see or yet imagine.

Amanita seemed to have accepted that she could not tempt Chanterelle with the soup. She lowered the bowl into her lap. "Shall I carry you downstairs, then?" she asked. "You would like to hear the music, I'm sure, and you'll hear it far better if you're in the room than you would from up here."

"Oh, yes. I do want to hear the music. I'd be very grateful if you'd carry me downstairs. I don't think I'll be able to walk for a day or two." As she said it, she realized that it was true. How, then, could she possibly do as her mother's shade had asked, and go to the secret place? Even if she had known where it was, how was she to get there?

Amanita put the bowl of soup down on the night-stand, and reached out to take Chanterelle in her arms. Chanterelle allowed herself to be picked up, very meekly.

Amanita took her down a wooden staircase, treading carefully, and into a spacious room brightly illuminated by twenty-four wax candles arranged in half a dozen candelabra, placed on tables or in brackets in each corner and half way along the longer walls. Twelve children, six boys and six girls, dressed neatly but simply, were arranged in two rows at one end of the room, like an improvised choir in a country church. In front of them, Catrianne was sitting on a curule chair, holding the famous kithara—which seemed to Chanterelle, who was seeing it for the first time, to be rather ordinary: simply an oddly-shaped frame with strings and pegs, a glorified lyre.

Amanita deposited Chanterelle on a sofa, beside her brother, and sat down on a large armchair beside the sofa, next to Chanterelle.

Catrianne had not quite finished tuning the instrument.

"You've been hunting?" Chanterelle whispered to Handsel.

"Yes," said Handsel. "It wasn't as exciting as I'd hoped. We couldn't keep up with the dogs, and could hardly see what they were chasing. They didn't catch anything. All we brought back was a basket of mushrooms."

"You didn't learn to see, then?" said Chanterelle, a trifle warily.

"It's funny you should say that," said Handsel, "because I did feel that I could see the forest mere clearly than I ever had during the last few days. It seemed more alive, greener and brighter. But Amanita says that it is—that this is the part of the forest that really does have an extra measure of life. That's what she's trying to preserve. I don't think she's wicked, not really. Callous, but not *evil*."

Chanterelle studied the children waiting patiently to sing. They were certainly not blind, in a literal sense, but they did seem to be entranced, in the grip of some kind of fascination. She had no doubt that they were here voluntarily, that they wanted to be here, that they liked being part of Amanita's nightingale choir…but she could understand why their parents might suspect that some kind of magic spell had been cast upon them, that they had been partly stolen.

"Don't expect too much," said Catrianne, as she prepared to play. "It's a long time since I played the instrument, and I haven't played one like it since. It will probably take weeks of practice before I've mastered it…but I think I can pick out a few tunes. Whether your children will know the words to them…."

"Don't worry about that," said Amanita. "Just play. Improvise. The children are used to doing the same, when I play."

Catrianne stated to play the melody that Handsel had picked out on the pipe he'd found in the forest, and Chanterelle saw her brother smile and pat the pouch attached to his belt, where he had stowed the pipe away. He hesitated for a moment, but then he took the tiny instrument out of the pouch. For the moment, however, he did not attempt to join in. Catrianne soon moved on to another familiar tune, another of Alastor's standard practice pieces, and then to a third.

It was during the third trial piece that the choir of children, having picked up the melody, began to sing—but not the words of the song that was associated with the tune in the town, or any other words. The children sang like birds, not whistling, as if in crude imitation of the chirping of birds, but singing wordlessly, making musical notes with their throats that mingled with the notes produced by the strings, and, after a few uncertainties, began to fuse with them.

Startled at first, Catrianne soon adapted her playing to that exotic style of accompaniment, and when she began to improvise, it was as if she were orchestrating for the voices, inviting an elaboration of her own chords in such a way as almost to specify the form it ought to take. And the children, even though they were only children, were able to rise to that challenge. They really had been trained, not merely to sing in harmony, but to sing as a choir, as a collective that was something more than the sum of its parts.

Then Handsel joined in too, on his pipe, and when Chanterelle looked at him, he saw that he too was entranced, if not by Amanita, then by the dream that the song had caught....or the dream that had caught the song.

Amanita was leaning forward avidly now, excited. "Yes, yes," she murmured. "That's it, that's it...."

Chanterelle had turned to look at her, and the fay met her gaze, triumphantly.

"You can hear it, can't you?" Amanita, whispered to her. "She had hardly been in the forest since childhood, and even then, it was only in the vicinity of the foundry, but what an ear she has! This is just a trial, a finger exercise...but you can already hear the wind in the branches, can't you, and the chorus of the birds? By the time your lovely aunt has mastered the kithara, she'll have had the song of the forest in her ears and her mind for days on end. Oh, Chanterelle, can you not hear it? Crude as it is, does it not make you want to join the song...to perfect the song...?" She fell silent again, and sat back in her armchair, closing her eyes in order to listen to the evolving song, and to savor it.

Chanterelle understood exactly what Amanita meant. She had never lived in the forest, and had only been traveling through it for a matter of days, barely making contact even with the parts of it in which Broceliande was already dead, but still, she understood what Amanita meant.

The forest, she knew, did have a song. The dream of Broceliande embodied a song, a song that must have been repetitive for most of the forest's unimaginably long lifetime, but was now seeking to improvise, seeking to change, without knowing exactly how it might be able to change, let alone how it might want to change…but in the meantime, its melody was being sung, by the wind in the crowns of the trees, and by the birds, by the birds most of all.

And Amanita was right. Chanterelle had no sooner heard the combination of Catrianne's playing and the human nightingales' singing than she felt a powerful temptation to join in, a desire to play her part in the improvisation, and share in its creativity and its guidance. She wanted to find the song of the forest, the song of Broceliande's dream, not merely to echo it, but to play an active part in it, to discover the song that it had not yet succeeded in becoming, but desperately yearned to become.

But she kept silent.

For all their careful training and the natural beauty of their voices, Chanterelle could tell that the human nightingales were not the right singers; for all her brilliance and intuition, Catrianne was not the right player; and for all the skill that her father had invested in it and all the ingenuity that Amanita had put into its design, the kithara was not the right instrument. They were all signposts to the way, but no more than that. It was all just a simulacrum, all just a deception, perhaps with good intentions, improvised with the only materials that had come to hand, but it was no more than that.

The real song, obviously, was the song of the forest itself, the authentic voice of Broceliande, and that was what was really behind the attraction that Chanterelle felt. The desire she felt increasing and blossoming within her was not a desire to sing to the kithara, accompanying Catrianne, in a room on Amanita's house. It was to sing in the last remaining nucleus of Broceliande, her real mother, with Lucinia.

Amanita sprang to her feet, furious—but not with Catrianne, whose playing was going from strength to strength, or the choir of children, whose members were working wonders, but because of another sound that had suddenly begun to interrupt the concert, and provide an additional accompaniment that was, to say the least, subversive.

Tap…tap…tap…

A huge hawk-moth was hurling itself repeatedly against one of the window-panes, doubtless attracted by the light inside the room, stupidly unaware of the fact that it could not get any closer to the multiple candle-flames that its compound eyes could glimpse within, like a vision of a lepidopteran paradise.

"Vandal!" muttered Amanita. "Abomination!" and she went to the window, and threw it open, not to let the importunate moth in, but in order to drive it away with broad sweeps of her slender arms and her long-fingered hands.

Catrianne continued playing, ignoring the distraction, and the children continued singing. The moth, frightened by Amanita's agitations, flew away. Handsel had not moved, except that his hand was still fidgeting about the pipe into which he was blowing, having been drawn to the music by the lure of the song.

But Chanterelle did move. Inspired by the song, and realizing at last what Broceliande wanted of her, what had been planned for her, even before she had been conceived, she rose from the sofa, testing her new-found wings and finding all the necessary reflexes already in place.

She was not a nightingale; having undergone metamorphosis, she was a swan. It was a swan that had to sing the song that, according to legend, swans sing. The legend was false, of course, in a literal sense, but the literal sense did not matter here; in the dream, myth was as sound as reality, and perhaps more plangent.

Amanita screamed in rage.

Chanterelle, having found her new form, flexed her long white neck and her huge white wings. Unlike a real swan she did not have to run over the surface of a lake in an ungainly fashion in order to attain the impetus to take off. She was a dream swan, and rose into the air with the same sinuousness and ease that had allowed her to glide through the forest undergrowth. Swiveling like a sylphide, she launched herself horizontally, and hurtled like an arrow through the open window and into the welcoming night, and flew into the darkness, toward the secret place.

XVI

Broceliande's Swan Song

"There you are, sister," said Lucinia, as the magical swan settled into her waiting arms, where she seemed to fit quite comfortably, although she would not have expected human arms to be capable of providing a safe refuge for a creature of her sort....whatever sort that was, beyond an appearance that already seemed to her to be a trifle unsteady.

Here I am, thought Chanterelle the swan. *But where? This is not how mother—Melusine—described the secret place in the story she told me"*

"No," admitted Lucinia, as if Chanterelle had formulated the thought in audible words. "It retained that appearance for a time, while I slept on what seemed to be a bed of moss, but was in fact a different kind of matter, the substance of which the figments of Broceliande's dreams were forged. I would have dissolved into that substance long ago, but I had to wait for you. I could not be sure that you would come, but I hoped. What alternative did I have?"

I still don't understand, Chanterelle thought, wistfully. *Every time I think I've almost gasped it, it changes again.*

"Dreams are like that, alas," said Lucinia. "I'll do my best to answer your questions, but there's only so much reason can do in trying to make sense of it, because there's always something, in music or in magic, that lies beyond the reach of reason."

Lucinia was not a day older than she had been when her mother, having used her own shapeshifting powers, carefully hoarded over the years, to rejuvenate her appearance and transfigure herself into a simulacrum of her daughter, had gone to wait for Alastor in the fissure in the rock, in order to depart with him for the distant town. Time had only taken its daily toll outside the space that she and Alastor has assisted Broceliande to prepare, when he had played the kithara there, she had sung, and Broceliande had dreamed with a concentration, a vividness and a lucidity that the mind of the forest had not previously contrived in hundreds of thousand of years.

Chanterelle no longer had a human voice, with which to form the syllables of the language with which she had grown up, but she had another voice now, adapted to form the syllables of the secret language in a fashion that no human larynx could contrive, and she tried hard to form them, if only for practice.

She had many questions, but it seemed to be enough, for the time being, to summarize them, economically, in a single syllable: "Why?"

"You should not hold it against our mother," Lucinia said. "She did what she thought was necessary. She wanted Alastor to father children with a fay, and she knew, although she had always denied it to her own kin, that I was only a demifay. It was me with whom Alastor had fallen in love, almost at first sight, and Melusine had no power of fascination sufficiently potent to alter that, but she did have the power of metamorphosis…or at least of casting a permanent glamor, and making a simulacrum. Deceiving Alastor was only a part of the plan; the real point was to deceive Amanita."

"Why?"

"To understand that, you need to understand what Melusine and Amanita were. They were the principal instruments by which the dying Broceliande, reaching for self-consciousness in the final crisis of her death-throes, sought to understand herself. Primarily, they were instruments of enquiry, intended to investigate human lore and to plunder any insight it had that might be useful. The pickings were thin, I fear, except in respect of the theory and artistry of music—but that was the necessary element, and one that might yet, perhaps be sufficient for Broceliande's needs as she now perceives them."

"Needs?"

"Broceliande understood—or perhaps *sensed* would be a better way of putting it, as understanding was something of which she was still in quest—that passive and placid enquiry is not a reliable way to reach the truth, that effective investigation requires antagonism and adversity, perpetual challenge and stern proof. Hence, she did not imagine one seeker of knowledge but two, who would be both collaborators and adversaries, sisters and competitors, who loved one another but were always at odds, even to the extent of accusing one another of wickedness and treason. That competition drove them, in the end to desperation, and even to bizarrerie…but that was what was necessary. It was, seen from one point of view, a mere reflection of Broceliande's agony, a kind of writhing; but it was also the action, and the thrust, from which a solution of sorts to the problem of her death might emerge. Perhaps it has, and perhaps not… only time will tell…but the time has come, for Amanita to make her effort, and for us—for you and I—to make ours."

"Us?"

"Our mother always knew that it would have to be the two of us who made that effort, because she knew that bearing more children, even children that were more fay than human, would condemn her to early death. She visited me in my dreams while I slept, to bring me news of the marriage to Alastor that she was living in my guise and in my stead, and news of the children that she bore. She expected to die soon enough, even before the advent of the plague that eventually killed her, and always told me that it was her love for Alastor—a love of which very few fays would have been capable—that kept her alive for so long. I'm quite certain that I could not have loved him half as well, for I, like Catrianne, find that kind of passion alien to my nature, although I believe that I could certainly have loved children…as I do, in fact, love you and Handsel, my sister and brother. I doubt, however, that Alastor could have loved the real me half as well as he loved the deceptive simulacrum."

"Me?"

"Doubtless you feel that you have been deceived too, but the mother with whom you lived, the mother who cared for you, really was your mother, even though she wore a false name. She did not tell Alastor or Handsel what they were because she was afraid that if she did, their subsequent investigations and behavior would make life untenable in the town, and she did not want you to return here to complete her plan until you were old enough to do so. Are you old enough now? I can't tell. Perhaps not…but time has run out. Although she had anticipated her own death, our mother had not anticipated Alastor's or the burning of his factory. She had, however, anticipated her sister's attack on the iron-master, although her principal anxiety in that regard was that Amanita might discover or deduce in the process that his children were demifays. She expected that, even if it was long after her death, Alastor would eventually bring you here when the time was ripe, in search of the secret place and of Melusine, never having realized that Melusine had exchanged herself for me."

"Me?"

"Perhaps you are also resentful about your own metamorphosis, but I fear that it cannot be reversed. I think, in fact, that in the context of Broceliande's dream, the symbolic swan has always been your true form, and that the one you have manifested thus far was always a temporary simulacrum. I can only hope that you might eventually feel comfortable with what you are, even though it is a blatant anomaly in the previous scheme of things. I can tell you, however, that you are by no means alone in being a bird capable of human thought and understanding, and might encounter others of your kind very soon, each of them one of a kind, beyond the scope of ancient nature. That is one of the strategies that the recently-conscious Broceliande had adopted in the hope of proving herself with an afterlife of sorts. The pure fae-folk will all die with her, but the demi-fays and metamorphs will retain within them something of the mentality of Broceliande, even if, in the fullness of time, it is only expressible in their songs, their dreams and their tales. That is one of several legacies that the dying forest hopes to leave behind."

"Several?"

"Indeed. I would like to believe that you and I are her best hope, and her most precious legacy, but who can tell? Amanita, I know, has conceived a new plan of her own, in addition to the attempt to influence the song of the forest with the aid of Catrianne, which she will doubtless continue for as long as she has breath in her body. My mother was never disappointed by the fact that she had Handsel first before giving birth to you. She glimpsed immediately the possibility that Amanita has only just perceived: that of Handsel having a child with a fay, whose posterity might be capable of preserving more of the mentality of Broceliande than that of any ordinary demifay. Melusine obviously did not have Amanita in mind as they fay in question, and probably considered her out of the question, in view of her long and determined virginity, but what alternatives are left? If Amanita is willing, as she seems to be....well she still has an appearance of youth, and Handsel has almost reached the threshold of adulthood. There might yet be time, if only just...."

"Just?"

"Is it just? Is any of this just? Is any of it *good?* Perhaps it is all wicked. Humans would certainly reckon it so, since they would reckon it all to be witchcraft, and hence the work of the Devil. Insofar as they have ever guessed or intuited the existence of Broceliande, they have always reckoned her a demon, a malign presence, and perhaps understandably, given that many of her once-prolific progeny, including Amanita, would have wiped out their entire human race had they been capable of doing so, as an act of vengeance as well as a possible means of saving the dream. Some of them would certainly have judged such an intention just, in accordance with the human principle of talion—an eye for an eye and a genocide for a genocide—but you and I need not concern ourselves with such abstract questions. Our role is to sing, and there is no justice or morality in song, but only beauty and emotion."

"Role?"

"Precisely. Our concern is more immediate and more intimate than anyone else's. Our role is to complete our mother's scheme: to provide the sustenance for the seed whose first element Alastor and I sowed fourteen years ago. Tonight, we will begin the consolidation and nutrition of that seed, and we shall continue it for as long as we are able. Eventually…and the time might not be far off…we shall become part of the seed ourselves, returning to the sleep in which I have been suspended for thirteen years, perhaps only for centuries, but perhaps for many millennia, awaiting the possibility of its germination, and the birth and growth of a new Broceliande, a daughter as beautiful, and more intelligent than her mother: a daughter capable of becoming conscious more rapidly, and more knowledgeable with very brief delay…possessed of every gift, in fact, that any mother would wish for her daughter, if circumstances permitted."

Chanterelle no longer had shoulders capable of shrugging in the fashion to which she was accustomed, but she had wings that could be flexed in imitation of that gesture. She did so, delighting in the sensation, intending to symbolize by that gesture and that rapture her acceptance of her new form and her new situation, her compliance with the plan that Broceliande had made for the continuation and eventual renewal of her dream, via the mind of Melusine, one of the figments she had engendered with that belated purpose in mind.

She thought, in the secret language: *Grandfather was perhaps not so mad after all to think that there might be a kind of peace and serenity in the mind of a bear or a wolf, whose self-consciousness is subdued by comparison with that of a human, and less subject to self-mortification. I am not a real swan, of course, but merely a near-fay in a fleshy form, but I wonder whether it might be reckoned a preferable form to the human form I wore before, and with which Amanita and Melusine were cursed in permanence. Form has its imperatives and its implications, after all, and if I am a symbolic swan, I can be all that a swan might symbolize, including beauty, purity and grace. And one day, when our duet is finished, I shall sleep, perhaps….just perhaps…to wake another day, in a new world; but even if the journey ends in oblivion, there will be dreams in the interim, and what dreams! Memory will allow me to dream that I am a human once again, and imagination will allow me to dream of being a hawk-moth, or a disincarnate soul, a messenger of eternity.*

She had begun to get a better sense now, of what and where they were. She and Lucinia seemed to be floating in darkness, but she knew that they were not floating in air, but in some other medium, composed of a different mater, perhaps located within the earth, but perhaps not even there, although they were still in some way juxtaposed with it. She and Lucinia, she thought, had enough of the human in them to retain that bond, perhaps even to visit the world of vulgar matter now and again… or at least to visit the dreams of the people becalmed there, including the people she loved.

But first, there was work to be done, and a task to complete.

And without wasting further time in reasoning, Chanterelle began to sing the first stanza of her swan song.

She began with the tune that Handsel had first picked out on the little pipe, and would doubtless pick out again in time to time, countless times, because it was the customary starting-point that example and experience had taught him. Then, like Catrianne testing the kithara, she began to explore other tunes that she had heard her father play when she was barely old enough to perceive a tune. And then, again like Catrianne, she began to improvise, to adapt her evolving song to the rhythm, the melody and the substance of Broceliande's ongoing dream, still evolving even on the point of death, still questing, still defiant.

And the chorus joined in.

The leader of that chorus, obviously, was Lucinia's human voice, which soared and swept, majestically and magnificently, sweeter and smoother than the voice that her simulacrum had contrived in imitation, and with which Chanterelle had so often sung in harmony before. But other voices joined in with Lucinia's too, from within and without the darkness within which they were no longer floating but flying, soaring and swooping, with a freedom that Chanterelle had never been able to imagine in her human form.

Some of the contributors to that chorus were doubtless metamorphs like Chanterelle herself, which had once worn human form for a while, but the majority were surely real birds, which had learned the songs of the forest as they had gone about their routine business of growth and reproduction. All of them joined in with the song of the forest, whether they had originated as figments of Broceliande's dream or not. All of them sang the same hymn, with all the artistry and enthusiasm of which they were capable, so that it not only filled the new dream that Broceliande was weaving, but the husk of the old one, the shell that had not yet been discarded.

It was a swan song, and was therefore plaintive, with the musical texture of a lament—but it was also triumphant, asserting the power of life even after and beyond death, asserting the conviction that all as not yet lost, in spite of the unwitting murder of a trillion cuts, in spite of the frailty of the dreaming mind.

And in the distance, in the house of brick and stone, Catrianne must have perceived at least a distant echo of it, for, having paused and put the kithara down, while the choir of children fell silent, she picked it up again, and began to play again. This time, when a host of hawk-moths came to tap upon the illuminated windows of the house, Amanita made no attempt to chase them way, but merely accepted their percussion as an element of the song.

And in the darkness of the ordinary night, the surviving fae-folk made magical white light, and the entire forest glimmered and gleamed, issuing a challenge to the cold and callous stars.

Meanwhile, in what had been the darkness of the secret place, a new light dawned, and Chanterelle and Lucinia, transfigured and transformed yet again, learned to see with new and previously-unimaginable eyes, not knowing whether an hour or a billion years had passed while they were lost in the song, but knowing that, in spite of everything, the light of life had once again blazed forth within the dream of death.

EPILOGUE

The New Year

Some months later than the evening when Chanterelle had flown away, in the dusk of first Monday after New Year's Day, Handsel, Amanita and Catrianne were walking in the wild forest by the light of the full moon. Two ghostly hunting-dogs were bounding alongside them, having no need of a leash to keep them under control.

Amanita was wearing her favorite cape of blood-red fur, flecked with black sequins. Handsel was wearing a fur cloak cut tailored from the hide of a brown bear, trimmed along the edges with the silkier fur of a gray she-wolf. The body of the fur was a flecked by mange in places, but the cloak was warm in spite of the spoiled patches. Catrianne was wearing a white full-length dress that reflected the moonlight with a beautiful silvery sheen.

"How beautiful the sylphs are as they dance on the moonbeams," Handsel said, "freshening the air with their agility."

"Indeed they are, my love," said Amanita.

"I like the dryads even more," said Handsel. "They know the very best of elfin music, and they love to play their pipes when the wind blows. I'm a poor piper by comparison, alas, and never did have Aunt Cat's talent for music. I hardly dare to accompany her when she invites me to do so Perhaps one should leave the exercise of such arts to those who know them best."

"Oh no," said Catrianne. "One should play for the simple pleasure of playing, as my brother, your father, always used to do."

"Indeed one should, my darling," said Amanita. "And Handsel is not nearly as poor a piper as he pretends. With a little education, he might yet produce the sweetest music."

"There is another song in the air tonight, is there not?" said Handsel, pausing suddenly and cocking his ear. "There is another voice, even more distant and more plaintive than the dryad pipes. I have heard it many a time before, but never by day and always very faint. What is it, do you think?"

"I think it might be is the song of a nightingale," said Amanita. "There must be a way to make them sing by day, I dare say, even if the horrid tale that humans tell is a lie."

"No," said Catrianne, who had a fine ear for birdsong as well as other kinds of music. "It isn't a nightingale, or any other familiar kind of bird. I've heard it before, while walking in the forest, but I cannot place it at all, and have never managed to catch a glimpse of the singer. Somehow, it conjures up the image in my mind of a swan, but that's absurd, as I know perfectly well that swans merely honk, and cannot sing at all. It's a mystery. Perhaps it's a bird unique to Broceliande. There seem to be a lot of those hereabouts, which could not be found in the dead woods in which I lived as a child, mere fodder for the ax and the raw material of charcoal"

It was Handsel who almost dared to voice the thought that had come to all their minds. "Perhaps…," he ventured.

"No, said Amanita, cutting him off. "Not that. She's far away by now, the little traitor, the foolish deserter, and will never return. If I had only managed to persuade her to take one more mouthful of soup…but it's water under the bridge, now. You must not think that we cannot be a happy family without her. We do not need her, since we do not have her, for if we did, Broceliande's dream would not have permitted her to fly away. The three of us can do what we need to do, for as long as we need to do it. We must, and we will, else our story would not end happily, and you know that all tales must end happily."

"Except…," Catrianne began, but immediately shut up.

"This," said Amanita, indicating herself, her two companions, and the dusk, "is the only ending possible, and the only one we need. Let us regret the departed, by all means, but let us focus our sight on the future—for we can see, can we not? We are the ones who can see clearly, through all the confusion."

"Yes," said Chatrianne, meekly. And she thought, in fact, that she *was* beginning to see clearly. She did not think that Amanita could prevail, in the end, in keeping the forest alive—but still, she might be able to do so for a while yet. And when Amanita died with the forest, as all the fae-folk would have to do, she, Catrianne, as a mere demifay, would simply become human, and she would be able to live on in Amanita's house, doubtless reputed to be a witch, but still alive, with a future of sorts before her.

Naturally, she had never said any of that to Amanita, who would not have considered it to be clear-sighted at all, but treasonous.

Handsel remained standing still for a moment longer, but then he shrugged his shoulders and resumed walking, when Amanita took his arm, in a fashion imitative of amorousness. That caused a frisson to run down Catrianne's spine, but only briefly. After all, why not?

"It's a pretty song that the bird is singing, though, isn't it, Aunt Cat?" said Handsel. "Given time, I think I'll be able to reproduce it on my flute, just as you can reproduce it on the kithara."

"It's the song of the forest itself," Catrianne agreed. "The one thing that will survive, perhaps, when all the rest of us are dead."

"Don't say that, my love," said Amanita. "We still have life, and beauty, to spare and to spend wisely, and we must make of it what we can. We must always strive to be as happy as we are now, and we must do our utmost to make all of this last forever. After all, what alternative do we have?"